THE COLLEC TORS

M. T. Anderson
e.E. Charlton-
Trujillo
DAVID LEVITHAN

THE
COLLEC
TORS

STORIES

CORY McCARTHY
ANNA-MARIE
McLEMORE
G. Neri

EDITED BY
A.S. KING

JASON REYNOLDS
Randy Ribay
JENNY TORRES
SANCHEZ

DUTTON
BOOKS

DUTTON BOOKS

An imprint of Penguin Random House LLC, New York

First published in the United States of America by Dutton Books,
an imprint of Penguin Random House LLC, 2023

The Collectors: An Anthology © 2023 by A.S. King
"Play House" © 2023 by Anna-Marie McLemore
"The White Savior Does Not Save the Day" © 2023 by Randy Ribay
"Take It from Me" © 2023 by David Levithan
"Ring of Fire" © 2023 by Jenny Sanchez
"Museum of Misery" © 2023 by Cory McCarthy
"La Concha" © 2023 by e.E. Charlton-Trujillo
"Pool Bandits" © 2023 by Greg Neri
"We Are Looking for Home" © 2023 by A.S. King
"A Record for Carole Before It All Goes" © 2023 by Jason Reynolds
"Sweet Everlasting" © 2023 by M. T. Anderson

Dutton is a registered trademark of Penguin Random House LLC.
The Penguin colophon is a registered trademark of Penguin Books Limited.

Visit us online at PenguinRandomHouse.com.

Library of Congress Cataloging-in-Publication Data is available.

ISBN 9780593620281

2nd Printing

Printed in the United States of America

LSCH

Design by Anna Booth
Text set in PT Serif Pro

For the weird ones and their weird friends

CONTENTS

THE COLLEC TORS

Introduction
A.S. King

Here is an incomplete list of things one can collect: crystals, lies, math tests, kittens, scraps of paper with things written on them, books, antiques, enemies, punctuation, friends, rumors, cars, feelings, baseballs, stepmothers, trophies, knowledge, joys, earbuds, anger, office supplies, judgments, conquests, opinions, insults, prophecies, dryer lint.

Collections are everywhere in human culture. Humans collect a lot of things. But why? *Why do we collect things?* I woke up from a dream with this question one day in 2021, and it followed me around until I did something with it. I started with research, but then I had to trust my gut.

There is science here—a psychology of collecting that has been studied by industry and academia through the lenses of economics and marketing to anthropology to neuropsychology and social psychology. Science tells us that collecting is ubiquitous, usually harmless, and normal, not to mention profitable. It tells us that a majority of children are collectors, as well as about 40 percent of adults, and it draws lines between healthy collecting and hoarding and other concerning behaviors. When asked, *Why do we collect things?* the data give us many answers depending on what's being collected, how it's being collected and shared, and in what culture the collecting is taking place. It's all very logical and tidy. But it doesn't feel true. While science is awesome, it lacks the nuance of artistic meaning, and that's part of why I think people collect things. I believe we collect what makes us feel good or what we're attracted to.

Collections are beautiful to their collectors. Even the most disgusting collection is a glimpse of magic to the right person. Same as the most boring collection can excite. Essentially, every collection is extraordinary and impossible to duplicate, because even if I have the same exact baseball cards as you do, mine hold a meaning for me that's different from yours. That individual meaning highlights the creative component—which tells me that collections are art, and the act of collection, artistry. Emotion trumps logic here. If you collect buttons/thimbles/rocks and you don't logically know why, I can tell you. You collect those buttons/thimbles/rocks because you're an artist and they somehow give life an extra layer of meaning for you. They make you happy.

I collect weird ideas. I collect weird stories. I collect weird questions. I write them on sticky notes and display them on my walls. For a few months, there was a blue sticky note above my desk. *Why do we collect things?* Next to it was a note from a year earlier that read, *Weird Short Story Collection.* You know what came next. You're holding it.

There is currency in weirdness that no one told me about when I was a young weird person. There is a freedom in it too. Once an artist can block out any suggestion to conform and let go of their own fear of failure, they have found a new place where dreams can come true. Additionally, when an artist allows themselves to get weird, they give permission to everyone else in the room to get weird with them.

This anthology of stories is the result of me asking nine of my favorite YA writers to write me a story about a collection and its collector, and asking them to toss out conventions, as there were no rules, there was no "normal," and they could be as weird as they wanted. *There is currency in weirdness,* I said. *Be defiantly creative,* I said. What they've created here is a new, beautiful collection of curiosity and hurting and growing up and healing and loving and living.

As you begin your journey through their words, I want to extend the same invitation to you, reader, for living your life and dreaming your dreams. There are no rules. There is no normal. You can be as weird as you want. Be defiantly creative. Make art of your life, especially if you don't consider yourself an artist—collect all the little pieces of you and make your story. When you look back many years from now, you will see something extraordinary and impossible to duplicate. You will see *you.*

Play House
by Anna-Marie McLemore

The first thing most people knew about Miranda Asturias was that Miranda Asturias had a beautiful mother. Miranda's mother had hair as black as her eyelashes. Her lip line was sharp and lent itself well to quick swipes of lipstick, so that the red looked painted as precisely as if she'd used a brush. Her skin was a brown as warm as August evenings in their neighborhood, the air between streetlights just damp enough to be filmy.

If Miranda's mother noticed the way men looked at her, she did not let on. Miranda's mother only noticed Miranda's father. Every morning in the kitchen, the two of them gazed at each other as though taking home the prize after a flawless draw of cards. So when Miranda's father, after a year out of work, got a job that would take him away for most of the summer, they looked as though something had been torn out of them, each of them cored like apples.

"You'll look after your mother, won't you?" Miranda's father asked her.

Miranda stood in the driveway and nodded. Then she heard herself say, "Wait," and ran into the house.

She came back with one of her glass bluebirds. It was small enough to disappear into her father's hand.

"For good luck," she said, though she'd just bought the bluebird at an estate sale the week before, and had no way of knowing.

As Miranda and her mother washed the dishes that night, there was something odd about the light outside, something knocked out of place. The evening was greener, and grayer, the kind that warned of tornados. But there were no sirens. Only the prickling sense of eyes watching the windows.

"Someone's out there," Miranda said.

Her mother laughed. "No, there's not."

But as the night deepened, the prickling grew stronger. Miranda could almost hear the eyes watching, gazes tapping on the glass like thrown pebbles.

"No, there's someone out there," Miranda said.

"Oh, querida." Her mother dried the last dish, set it on the stack in the cupboard. She lined up the scalloped edge perfectly with the one underneath. "Stop. You'll give yourself bad dreams."

Miranda's mother did not seem to realize she was a famous beauty. She did not seem to notice how men looked at her. And this was unfortunate. Because if she had, she might have believed Miranda. They both might have felt in the air what was coming next.

· · · · · · · · · · · · ·

At first, it was a couple of neighbors, men Miranda had seen greeting her father as he pruned the azaleas. One sat in a chair at the kitchen table. Another took up residence on the north end of the sofa. A third sat in the frayed armchair he must have assumed was her father's favorite. The men came quickly, that night and the next morning, as though they'd been waiting in the shadows of the trees for her father's car to vanish down the road.

"You two girls need a man in the house," each proclaimed. Each tried to elbow the others out of the way. Each tried to shove ahead to get the first glass of agua de frambuesa, because her mother felt obligated to offer something to these men, who were technically guests, even though they had never rung the front doorbell.

"Don't give them things," Miranda told her mother as they stood at the kitchen sink. The kitchen sink seemed to be one of the few places she and her mother could talk without the men lifting their chins to listen. At the kitchen sink, the men assumed they were talking of nothing but dishwashing liquid and scouring pads.

"If you give them things," Miranda said, "they'll stay."

"They're our neighbors," her mother said. "We have to be polite." She tried to give Miranda the kind of soft smile she gave everyone. But a tendon in her neck stood out, taut as the gusset on the refrigerator. Light freckled her face, the sharp glare of the morning punching holes in the lace curtains.

. . . .

The things that made Miranda's mother not just a beauty but a famous one were her eyes. They were green, and against the brown of her skin, they were startling in both their paleness and brightness. They were the color of bridesmaids' dresses in shades called "seafoam" or "mermaid." They were the mint green of the appliances that were in all the catalogs fifty years ago and were everywhere again now.

If it hadn't been her eyes, it would have been the way she never seemed to get anything on her dresses, even clouds of powdered sugar for Christmas cookies, even the hot red spray off the Asturias family recipe for arroz. She did not wear aprons. She did not need them.

Miranda was always getting things on her clothes, especially while cooking with her mother. Especially in the summer. In the summer, she and her mother pulled blackberries from the sweet relentless brambles behind the house, the ones forever trying to swallow the garden shed whole. Her mother stirred dark jam on the stove, and the fine spray off the boiling pots always seemed to find Miranda.

This was how the apron collection started. Each came from the same garage sales and estate sales where Miranda found her glass bluebirds, wandering the yards of the living and the houses of the dead. If the deceased was a woman above a certain age, there was al-most certain to be a bluebird or aprons or both. Miranda's closet now held a fluttering array of aprons, each faintly stained. Tomatillo on the one patterned with candy corn, and on the one with the peonies. Mole rojo on the one printed with holly leaves, and the red plaid. Blackberry on the one with the cherry pattern, and the one with the whimsically angled cupcakes.

This morning, Miranda came early to the estate sale, as soon as the house opened. She always came early, but especially now. There was less chance of encountering the men's wives. The wives glared at Miranda and her mother whenever they saw them, as though they had stolen their husbands. Miranda would have baked them all pan dulce leavened with her own gratitude if only they would come and take their husbands back.

Miranda could tell from the smell in the deceased woman's house that she had had a signature perfume, deep and golden and shimmery. It permeated the air between her pieces of dark-finished furniture. Miranda imagined a woman who wore red agate rather than pearls, and who might have owned neither aprons nor glass bluebirds. But Miranda found two glass bluebirds on a carefully dusted shelf—one bright as Easter egg dye, one a little greener like her mother's eyes. And two aprons flopped over a dining room chair. The first apron repeated a delicate scene of frolicking deer in green toile, like an Austrian fairy-tale forest. The second had mallard ducks that looked so tacky in contrast, it made both aprons even more perfect.

Miranda bought the bluebirds from the woman's daughters, and asked how much for the aprons.

"Oh." One of them laughed, showing the bluish and lemon-hued stains on the fabric of each. "Just take them."

. . . .

More of them came.

"It's not safe to be on your own like this," the men said.

They filled the other chairs at the kitchen table. They fought for places on the sofa. They put their feet up on the windowsills. They crowded the fridge and freezer doors with their beers and liquor bottles.

Miranda barely told the men apart. One face blurred into the next, each ghostly pale in the gray-green evenings. When she did tell them apart, it was by what they drank. Budweiser, meant to prove they were real men, the crushed cans strewn like dry leaves. Vodka that smelled as strong as cleaning solvents. Jugs of grocery-store wine as big as gallon milk bottles. And one who jealously guarded a fifth of green Italian liquor that he seemed to think would impress her mother. But her mother gave the wan smile that was becoming her default expression, and turned away.

The green liquor was mint-flavored, so the man smelled perpetually as though he'd just swallowed mouthwash, covering the stink of cigarettes and her mother's cooking in his mouth. The man had come from a few streets over, and had not gone home since arriving. Miranda only knew this because his wife had banged on the door at three in the morning, calling, "Wyatt! Wyatt, I know you're in there." And the name startled Miranda because Wyatt had insisted that Miranda and her mother call him River, since his favorite movie actor had been called River.

"It'll be your and your mother's special name for me," he told them, like the kind of man who wanted to be referred to as "uncle" right after introducing himself.

That was what started it, his nicotine-mint breath on her skin, on her new apron printed with frolicking deer. That was the day Miranda started moving things to the garden shed. Things she did not want the men in the house to touch. Things she did not want permeated with the smell of liquor and crushed metal.

She started with her aprons. She cleaned a bent coatrack that had been left in the garden shed when her parents bought the house, and looped the apron ties over the hooks. There were a number of disused things the previous owners had left, and now Miranda used them. She dusted a bookshelf tilting from the warped wood. She cleaned an old dresser that was missing a drawer. Once the tops shone with wood polish, she placed her collection of glass bluebirds, including the two new ones from the dead woman who wore the golden perfume.

· · · · · · · · · · · ·

The men in the house said wasn't it time Miranda's mother started on dinner, and they came to a consensus about what they wanted, steak and eggs this time. Her mother gently suggested that wouldn't their wives be expecting them home for dinner? The men said that their wives understood that they were doing a good thing, looking out for a woman and her daughter who did not have a man in the house.

"But we do," Miranda whispered to her mother. "He's just not here."

The smell of splattering grease mixed with the lemon of the dish soap, pitting Miranda's stomach.

"Please," Miranda said to her mother. "Make them leave."

The men watched her mother at the stove. They watched the shape of her, how she moved, how her skirts moved. Her dresses—most of them cap-sleeve, the waists cinched, the skirts blooming with layers— all came in tasteful shades of brown, black, navy. Her chin-length hair was softly curled and set, red-painted fingernails tucking stray loops behind her ears.

"Or I'll do it," Miranda said. "I'll do it. Can I make them leave?"

Her mother looked at her, not quite looked at her. She looked almost at her but mostly out the window.

"Nice neighborhoods like this," her mother said, "they don't want people like us here. That's why we have to be nicer, more polite, more put together. To prove we belong here. Do you see, mija? We have to be better than them."

Now her mother did look at her, her face pretty and powdered and tense and hopeful. And in that expression, that unspoken *Please?* Miranda heard all the rest.

It wasn't as though Miranda had never thought about this. There was no way not to notice how, when her family walked down the street, blond mothers gathered blond children out of front yards and into their doorways. The neighbors looked at them with uneasy concern, as though they were each a blight on the wide-lawned lane. Her mother, a broken streetlamp, all jagged glass. Her father, a downed tree, leaning heavy on an electrical line. Miranda, a pothole, filling with asphalt-sour rain.

To live in such a neatly painted house, on a road where all the streetlamps worked, where all the trees had perfect posture, where the asphalt had been so recently repaved that it looked like a dark river, they had to be lovely and agreeable. They had to offer galletas to anyone who walked in the door even when they didn't knock.

· · · · · · · · · · · ·

The longer the men stayed, the more Miranda took out to the garden shed. The golden tubes of her mother's lipsticks, the ones her mother didn't use except to go out with Miranda's father. The petaled skirts of her mother's favorite spring and summer dresses, the ones her mother didn't wear except to go out with Miranda's father. The set of wooden darning mushrooms; the three of them had painted the plain tops red with white spots so they looked like amanita.

The land itself seemed to approve. The purple cotton candy of butterfly bushes framed the creaking shed door. Wood sorrel sprouted a ring around the shed, the shamrocks so brilliantly green and perfectly Irish that they looked fake. The blackberry brambles rose up protectively, as though guarding Rapunzel's tower.

· · · · · · · · · · · ·

River-not-Wyatt caught Miranda leaving the kitchen. He showed her pictures of the actor named River, asking, "Don't I look like him? Don't you think I look like him?" and wouldn't stop until Miranda gave enough of a vague nod to satisfy him, so he'd get out of the way.

"It's a shame about the brown." River-not-Wyatt pointed at her face, right at the bridge of her nose. "It's a shame you got those. You could've had your mother's eyes."

Miranda tried to step back, but a tension pulled on her.

River-not-Wyatt had grasped the corner of her apron, one of the mallard ducks pinched between his thumb and forefinger.

. . . .

The more Miranda took, the more the shed looked less like a shed and more like a playhouse, fit with all the things a girl needed to pretend cook or serve tea to stuffed animals. It didn't look complete without the Tupperware from the kitchen, so she took them, the Wonderliers in candy brights. And if she took the Wonderliers, it made sense to take her favorite cookbooks, the pages ruffled with sugar and syrup.

Here, Miranda hid the evidence of her and her mother's beautiful lives. Here, she could wear a frilled apron and a swipe of her mother's lipstick without the men watching. Here, she did not need to be nice to anyone. And it was enough that when her father called and asked how she and her mother were, she told him, "We're fine, Papá, everything's fine."

River-not-Wyatt may have kept following her around, showing new pictures of the actor, asking didn't she see it, how could she not see the way River-not-Wyatt looked just like him. Miranda's mother may have been silent in the kitchen, moving slowly as a sleepwalker. But the bluebirds and the Wonderliers were safe, and that was a start.

. . . .

All this—the things she'd hidden away from the men's fingers and eyes, the approving tilt to the blackberry vines and the butterfly bushes—made her bold. So she put on the green toile apron, the one with the deer.

River-not-Wyatt stopped her on her way to the back door. He wanted to know where his good Italian liquor was. From the smell on his breath, it was all down his throat. But he kept asking the other men, and the other men kept laughing, at or despite him.

"One of them took it." River-not-Wyatt gripped Miranda's arm, pinning a loose apron ribbon to her sleeve. "What does your mother let all of them in here for? She doesn't need them. I'm here."

Miranda swatted his hand away, hard enough that River-not-Wyatt stepped back.

The men let out a collective theatrical sound as though River-not-Wyatt had just been called to the principal's office. Their shared exhalation of breath made the air smell even more sharply of beer.

Miranda went out to the garden shed and the glint of gold lipstick tubes. She went out to the family of bluebirds the colors of sea glass. She went out to the perfume bottles she was keeping safe for her mother, to the candy-bright Tupperware bowls and her coatrack full of aprons with their edges frilled like peonies.

She did not realize he was there until she heard his voice, the hard, clipped "Hey" a barked-out objection. But even that one syllable slurred, dripping into the air.

Miranda turned, back against the garden shed wall. River-not-Wyatt was scratched up from the blackberry brambles. But he didn't seem to notice, and the pale scratches didn't bleed. The bright green of crushed wood sorrel and the purple fluff of trampled butterfly bush stuck to his shoes.

"You don't know what a good thing I'm doing for you and your mother." Each word ran like wet newsprint. "I don't think you're really appreciating how I'm looking out for the both of you."

He stepped far enough into the shed to reach the dresser. He grabbed one of the glass bluebirds and threw it down as though skipping a stone across a pond. Miranda's hand grasped the air, trying to catch it, but it fell too fast. Starbursts of glass, bright as a blue Popsicle, flew over the shed floor.

Miranda opened her mouth to scream at him. But her throat snapped closed like the lid on a lipstick tube, like the seal on a Wonderlier. Her hand was still grabbing at the air, reaching for the glass bird that had already broken.

Then her other hand moved. The flashes of mint green on her fingernails shimmered to life. She did not understand what her other hand meant to do until it shoved River-not-Wyatt. When she understood, she helped it. She pushed harder. She didn't care where it landed. His face. His shoulder. His stomach. She just wanted to shove him away.

So she jammed her weight forward. She sent all the force of her body into that hand. It landed on his arm, and he stumbled back. She was illuminated with spite and anticipation. He would land on the broken glass he'd just made. What was left of that bird would bite him back.

But he did not fall. She did not manage to shove him away. At least not all of him. Most of him stumbled back, but a piece of him was left in her hand. A chunk of his arm had broken off, but there was no blood or flesh. There was a glazed finish instead of skin. There was the pale crumble of broken ceramic instead of muscle. There was no blood, and no blood on River-not-Wyatt either. He was gripping the hollow of rough, pale ceramic that had opened in his once-perfect arm.

For a second, he looked as surprised as Miranda. It didn't last. His expression twisted with offense. Before she could even offer the broken piece back to him, he was running toward the house, ramming through the brambles.

This was it. It was over. He would yell to the whole neighborhood that Miranda and her mother were the vilest kind of women and that their house was a cursed place that turned men's bodies into painted figurines. They did not belong here, and he would tell everyone.

The piece of River-not-Wyatt was still in Miranda's hand. It grew heavy enough that she had to carry it in both palms. She followed him, holding it out. They had glue somewhere, didn't they?

The brambles parted with gentlemanly languor, as though opening a door for her, and Miranda heard what River-not-Wyatt was yelling. "Do you see what she's done to me? Do you see what she's like? I didn't do anything, and this is what she did to me."

By the time Miranda got to the back door, they were all looking at her.

She stood at the frame, holding the broken piece.

Her mother had been right all along. They would lose everything, all because Miranda had not smiled and brought them sandwiches.

The men's bottles and cans and cigarettes went still. Miranda waited for their faces to match River-not-Wyatt's. Appalled. Outraged.

But their expressions turned stricken and horrified, as though Miranda were showing off a living organ.

So she held it that way. She displayed it as though she had deliberately cracked it right off a man's arm. Her throat still would not give, would not release its Wonderlier seal. But she held this chunk of River-not-Wyatt, and she stared at the other men, unblinking, and it was loud as a scream. They scrambled out of chairs and off sofas, watching her, gauging the sharpness of her painted fingernails. They ran from the house, looking back as though she might run after them and rip their livers or lungs from their bodies.

When there was no one left in the room but River-not-Wyatt, Miranda stared at him with that same unblinking glare.

She held the piece of his arm out to him.

He ran without taking it.

. . . .

Miranda waited for her mother to remind her that they must be polite, welcoming. She waited for it as they gathered up the crushed cans, the bottles, the abandoned plates. As they washed the dishes. As they laundered the curtains grayed with cigarette ash.

But her mother said nothing of it. Miranda was not even sure she knew what had happened until she dusted the figurines on the high shelves, and gave Miranda a smile as wry and wicked as a secret.

Miranda took the broken piece of River-not-Wyatt outside. She left it in the front yard, his painted skin and his pale, crumbling flesh a warning before the front door.

The next time they made mole rojo, Miranda wore the apron with the mallard ducks, and the cooking stained it red. Miranda didn't notice until they were done that her mother had gotten a slash of mole rojo on her own blouse. She didn't change the blouse before they took a walk that night, so Miranda didn't take off her apron either. They went out that way, their heels clicking against the sidewalks, the men backing away from them as though they were streaked in blood.

The White Savior Does Not Save the Day
by Randy Ribay

CUT TO:

EXT. COASTAL CITY ON A PACIFIC ISLAND—DAY

A siren wails through an empty Southeast Asian city where clusters of buildings cling to a picturesque, crescent-shaped coastline. Along an abandoned beach, palm trees sway beneath a stormy sky and vacant fishing boats sit in an eerily placid gray bay. In the distance, a low rumble.

CUT TO:

INT. SCHOOL BUILDING—DAY

Generic Southeast Asian CHILDREN and their generic Southeast Asian TEACHERS scream and cry. They are very brown-skinned. They are desperately attempting to escape the building, but their efforts are in vain—a mysterious force has sealed all exits, trapping everyone inside. As they yell for help in some unstranslated language, one CHILD stares fearfully out a window facing the sea.

CUT TO:

EXT. SCHOOL BUILDING—DAY

Generic Southeast Asian RESCUERS struggle to open the front door of the school. They work with a calm urgency, occasionally stealing glances at the water.

CUT TO:

EXT. SEA—DAY

On the horizon, a wave. At first, there's no frame of reference to gauge its size. But as it approaches, the crest dwarfs an industrial fishing boat and easily sweeps the vessel into its swell—a tsunami.

CUT TO:

INT. SCHOOL BUILDING—DAY

The CHILDREN and TEACHERS continue panicking as they scream and bang on the doors. A TEACHER tosses a chair at a window, but the window does not even crack.

CUT TO:

EXT. SCHOOL BUILDING—DAY

RESCUERS determinedly work to force open the front door with a Jaws of Life tool. Though their efforts seem futile at first, the metal eventually starts to bend.

CUT TO:

EXT. SEA—DAY

The rumble grows louder as the tsunami nears. Its expansive first wave begins to break, with whitecaps at least forty or fifty feet high, swallowing the boats stuck out at sea.

CUT TO:

EXT. SCHOOL BUILDING—DAY

The RESCUERS pry open the front doors of the school enough to see the panicked faces of the CHILDREN inside. Using all their strength, they crank the tool and widen the opening inch by inch until it's large enough for people to pass through. A RESCUER reaches out an open hand to begin the evacuation.

As the first CHILD is about to take the hand, the building suddenly begins to tremble, knocking everyone off their feet. As it continues shaking, there's a deep groaning from beneath the ground and then the sound of concrete cracking. The RESCUER turns to look over his shoulder, expecting to see that the tsunami is upon them, that they've failed.

CUT TO:

EXT. SEA—DAY
The massive tsunami is closer but still some distance away from the shore.

CUT TO:

EXT. SCHOOL BUILDING—DAY
Confusion sweeps over the RESCUER's face. He turns back to the school building—but it's gone. In its place: a crater veined with broken pipes and torn wires. He is confused. But then another RESCUER points upward at the school building, ripped from the ground like an uprooted plant, somehow flying through the air.

CUT TO:

INT. SCHOOL BUILDING—DAY
The CHILDREN and TEACHERS press their faces to the windows. Their fear turns to confusion as they fly out over the sea, leaving behind the danger of the tsunami.

CUT TO:

EXT. SCHOOL BUILDING—DAY

WHITE SAVIOR is carrying the building from below as she soars through the air. Her white cape flutters in the wind, and her yellow hair flows perfectly behind her head like a golden comet's tail. Her glowing blue eyes focus on the horizon. Thanks to her superhuman strength, carrying the building causes her no strain. However, she seems exhausted, as if she's had a long day.

Eventually, she sets the building down in an open field and tears the front doors open the rest of the way. WHITE SAVIOR smiles and waves as the generic Southeast Asian CHILDREN and TEACHERS emerge from the building, blinking into the sunlight. They are very brown-skinned.

WHITE SAVIOR

Don't worry, you're safe now.

A TEACHER steps forward and asks something in a foreign language.

WHITE SAVIOR

You want a selfie, I suppose. I'm in a bit of a rush . . .
but okay.

WHITE SAVIOR takes out her phone, snaps a selfie with the generic Southeast Asians in the background, and uploads it to her feed. As the teacher continues trying to talk to her, WHITE SAVIOR waves goodbye and takes to the air.

CUT TO:

EXT. SKY—DAY

WHITE SAVIOR soars through a blue sky. Her smile fades, replaced by weary determination. She touches a finger to the communicator in her ear.

> **WHITE SAVIOR**
>
> I saved the school from the tsunami, LBB4. Are the missionaries from the Canadian orphanage on their way to pick up the kids?

> **LITTLE BROWN BROTHER #4**
> **(v.o. with a strong Filipino accent)**
>
> Yes, WS, but their parents have been calling—

> **WHITE SAVIOR**
>
> Great, they'll end up in good homes. On my way to Tanzania for the elephants next. Have you located Big Brain yet?

> **LITTLE BROWN BROTHER #4**
>
> The Tanzanian conservancy groups have also been reaching out, WS. They'd like to reiterate that placing all the elephants in zoos is not the best solution to the—

> **WHITE SAVIOR**
>
> Focus, LBB4—Big Brain?

LITTLE BROWN BROTHER #4

[Sighs] Yes, but first you should rest. You've been saving people nonstop for a week! You can't keep this up.

WHITE SAVIOR

These people can't save themselves, LBB4. And we know Big Brain's behind *everything*—from invalidating all the boba tea gift cards we distributed to the homeless of Mexico City, to trapping those poor Malaysian kids in that school, to providing tech to these Tanzanian poachers. I can't stop until I stop him.

LITTLE BROWN BROTHER #4

But maybe he's wreaking all this havoc because he *wants* you to go to him, WS. Maybe it's a trap.

WHITE SAVIOR

It doesn't matter. It's the only way.

LITTLE BROWN BROTHER #4

[Sighs] Fine. Sending you the coordinates now . . .

CUT TO:

EXT. SCHOOL BUILDING—DAY
The generic Southeast Asian CHILDREN and TEACHERS look around, puzzled as to how they're going to get home.

FADE OUT.

. . . .

Perdita Padilla sits cross-legged in the darkness on her bed, glasses on, long black hair down, face lit by the glow of her laptop. In the surrounding shadows, *White Savior* figurines line her shelves, *White Savior* posters hang on her walls, and *White Savior* T-shirts fill her dresser drawers.

It's late. She should be asleep. Instead, she's idly scrolling through the vintage script collectors' forum.

Again.

It's a waste of time, though. And she knows it. Perdita has several alerts set up to notify her the instant *White Savior* merch is posted anywhere on the internet. There's one variation specifically scanning for any mention of the TV show's finale script. It's the only one from the series she doesn't have. The one that might help everything make sense.

The show was canceled abruptly back in 2010, when the lead actress, Jennifer de Luca, inexplicably disappeared. Most speculated that she slipped away and changed her name to escape the limelight, maybe even to her husband's home country of the Philippines. However, others rightly pointed out that she wasn't even that well-known—the show had never even broken the top ten in the Nielsen ratings for its time slot. It was more likely she broke her contract in some way and the studio quietly let her go.

Whatever the reason, the final episode never aired. It was never even filmed. The only way for anyone to know how everything concluded, then, would be to read the script. Except nobody in the world could find a single copy or could remember ever seeing one.

There's a soft knock at the door.

"Yeah?" Perdita says, but she already knows who it is.

The door cracks open enough to reveal her stepmom's freckled face. The woman is smiling in that annoying way she has of conveying way too much gentle concern.

"Still up?"

"No. I'm sound asleep." Perdita turns her attention back to the forum.

"It's a school night, honey."

Perdita shrugs. Adjusts her glasses. Scrolls. "I have straight As, don't I?"

Her stepmother sighs. She can't argue with that. "Just try to get some rest soon, okay?"

Perdita doesn't respond.

"Love you."

Perdita doesn't respond.

The door softly closes. Muffled footsteps fade away.

As Perdita expects, a few moments later she hears the quiet sound of her stepmother's voice coming through the vent that connects her and her parents' bedrooms. Convenient sometimes. Other times . . . not so much.

"She was on her computer," her stepmother says.

"Probably looking for more *White Savior* shit," comes her dad's voice, uninterested, resigned.

"Doesn't her obsession ever strike you as more than a little . . . unhealthy?"

"It makes sense, though."

"Does it? Even at this age?" There's a long silence, then Perdita's stepmother adds, "You should talk to her."

"And say what—that she should throw all that stuff away and grow up?"

"Not in those exact words, but sure, something along those lines. And it might be worth mentioning therapy."

"You actually think that would work?" her dad asks.

"I don't know. But she's a teenager. She should be doing teenager-y things. Not spending all her time obsessing over a canceled children's TV show."

"You know it's more than that to her."

Her stepmom lets out a brief, sarcastic laugh. "You're really content to let her continue living with this . . . fantasy?"

"There's nothing we can do. Besides, she's not hurting anyone, and she's doing fine in school. She'll outgrow this all eventually."

"You're always saying that, but just last week, I asked her if she understood that all that stuff in the show wasn't real. Want to know what she said?"

"Not really."

"She asked me how we know anything is real."

Perdita's dad sighs.

"She needs professional—"

Perdita reaches over to her nightstand for her noise-canceling headphones and slips them over her ears. She pulls up a random episode of *The White Savior*, hits play, and settles in to watch. It's the one where White Savior saves a Native American community from extinction by leading them to victory in a lacrosse tournament against aliens. A classic.

Of course she knows the show is fake. The special effects budget left much to be desired.

But when Perdita watches the show like this—lights off, late at night, alone in her room and feeling lost—there's a part of her that wonders, that feels like she's glimpsing something real. Or, at least, something slightly out of focus. Something that might help everything else make sense if she could only make sense of it.

Before the episode reaches the end of the first act, her computer pings with a new email—it's one of the auto-alerts.

The lost script.

· · · · · · · · · · · ·

FADE IN:

EXT. SPACE STATION—NIGHT

WHITE SAVIOR, carrying LITTLE BROWN BROTHER #4, lands at the entrance of a large, ominous-looking space station. LITTLE BROWN BROTHER #4 is a short Filipino boy with a bowl cut. He's wearing a space suit, his laser escrima sticks sheathed like an X across his back. His eyes are wide with fear, as if he knows he's out of his league. WHITE SAVIOR sets him down, then steps back and examines the large metallic doors. She tries to pry them open, but they don't budge.

WHITE SAVIOR

Can you hack it?

LITTLE BROWN BROTHER #4 nods. He goes to the control panel and begins rapidly hitting keys.

LITTLE BROWN BROTHER #4

If your powers aren't working, WS, that means Big
Brain must be near.

WHITE SAVIOR

My powers are fine. Just get that door open, LBB4.

LITTLE BROWN BROTHER #4

If you say so.

There's a series of BEEPS, then the doors WHOOSH open, revealing a long, empty corridor lit by two parallel strips of glowing white lights. WHITE SAVIOR steps inside, trailed by LITTLE BROWN BROTHER #4. The doors close behind them.

CUT TO:

INT. SPACE STATION—NIGHT

WHITE SAVIOR and LITTLE BROWN BROTHER #4 walk down the corridor. It is eerily quiet save for the steady hum of the space station's hidden machinery. WHITE SAVIOR strides confidently ahead, but LITTLE BROWN BROTHER #4 unsheathes and activates his laser escrima sticks. Except nobody appears. No henchmen. No minions. No attackbots.

WHITE SAVIOR

Interesting.

LITTLE BROWN BROTHER #4

This is for sure a trap, WS.

WHITE SAVIOR

Shall we spring it?

LITTLE BROWN BROTHER #4
I'd rather we didn't, lest I end up like my predecessors.

WHITE SAVIOR ignores him, and they proceed down the creepily vacant hallway. The tension builds as the pathway turns—but nobody's around the corner. They follow the corridor as it twists and turns a few more times, revealing only emptiness.

LITTLE BROWN BROTHER #4
I don't feel great about this, WS. Disabling Big Brain's satellites ended his ability to create that nonstop chaos, just as I predicted it would. We don't need to be here.

WHITE SAVIOR
But what about Big Brain's next plan?

LITTLE BROWN BROTHER #4
This isn't about stopping Big Brain, is it?

WHITE SAVIOR
Of course it is.

LITTLE BROWN BROTHER #4
This is about . . . your daughter.

LITTLE BROWN BROTHER #4 stops walking. WHITE SAVIOR does not.

LITTLE BROWN BROTHER #4
He killed her, yes—but there's no bringing her back.

You must move on, or this desire for revenge will consume you.

WHITE SAVIOR holds her stony silence and continues walking, but her eyes well with tears held back. LITTLE BROWN BROTHER #4 shakes his head and jogs to catch up.

A few moments later, they turn one last corner and find themselves at another set of large metallic doors. Again, WHITE SAVIOR tries and fails to pry them open. LITTLE BROWN BROTHER #4 sheathes his sticks and gets to work hacking the control panel without being asked. After a few moments, there's a series of BEEPS and the doors WHOOSH open. He smiles, then turns to the open doorway. His smile falls.

CUT TO:

INT. CONTROL ROOM—NIGHT

BIG BRAIN sits on a floating throne in the middle of the inner room, surrounded by control panels, wearing an ostentatious supervillain outfit with a dramatically high collar. He is a middle-aged white man with an oversized head that pulsates red beneath a thin comb-over. He smirks, winks, and shoots a laser from the center of his forehead.

CUT TO:

INT. SPACE STATION HALLWAY—NIGHT

The laser hits LITTLE BROWN BROTHER #4 and he explodes. Blood, guts, and bits of flesh shower WHITE SAVIOR, staining her white suit and dyed blond hair crimson. Her blue eyes go wide with shock. A moment later, anger arrives. Her jaw sets. Her fists clench. She wipes blood from her face and shifts her attention back to BIG BRAIN.

WHITE SAVIOR

You promised you wouldn't kill this one.

CUT TO: BLACK

. . . .

A small bell above the door jingles as Perdita steps inside BB's Vintage Toy Dungeon. Even though she's never been here, it's just like all the other sad, dimly lit strip-mall storefronts crammed with collectibles. The smell of ancient plastic, sunlight-bleached cardboard, and basement-dweller body odor hangs in the air. Old action figures, comics, games, and memorabilia organized by franchise crowd narrow aisles. Cheap five-for-whatever toys fill bins that sit on the floor while the stuff worth actual money lines the shelves near the ceiling, still in its original packaging. However, the most valuable items are likely kept in the back, out of sight.

Buzzing with excitement and grateful that the vendor turned out to be only an hour's drive away, Perdita beelines to the glass counter in the back of the store. Nobody's behind the register, though. There's a closed door that probably leads to the stockroom, which is where the owner might be.

"Excuse me?" Perdita calls, disappointed but not surprised. These kinds of places rarely have any employees beyond the owner. "I'm the one who emailed you about the *White Savior* script?"

She waits a moment. There's no response. No movement from within.

She tries again, louder: "Hello? Anybody?"

Still nothing.

Perdita sighs, then wanders the store to kill time. However, there's no script or rare book collection out on display, and their *White Savior* section contains nothing she doesn't already own. She returns to the counter. After calling out again to no answer, she drops her gaze to the rare collectible trading cards in in the display case that serves as the counter. She taps her fingers on the glass and wonders why anyone would spend so much money on a game meant for children.

Perdita's completely aware that someone might say the same of her *White Savior* obsession. But that's different. Logical. Besides, she doesn't plan on paying full asking price for the script. She might if she could afford to, but she's never even seen that much money. Instead, after confirming that the script is real, Perdita will do what she always does to obtain the necessary discount—she will explain why the White Savior means so much to her.

She will explain that the White Savior was her mother.

Rather, the actress who played the White Savior—Jennifer de Luca—was her mother.

The rest of the encounter would play out like a script of its own. The vendor would be skeptical given the actress's whiteness and Perdita's ethnic ambiguity. But Perdita would show a few curated pictures on her phone: her mom in the hospital bed, love-drunk as she cradled a newborn Perdita; her mom holding a nine-month-old Perdita's hands on the beach as she attempted to walk; her mom kissing Perdita's Filipino father while a two-year-old Perdita sat laughing atop his shoulders. The vendor, finally convinced, would ask what *really* happened to Jennifer de Luca. Perdita's eyes would well with tears, and she would admit—truthfully—that she wished she knew. Then the vendor would either give Perdita the *White Savior* item for free or at a steep discount.

However, Perdita cannot help but feel that this time isn't about acquiring one more piece of merchandise. The script is the key. It's the end of her mother's story. And it's as much closure as Perdita can probably ever hope to get so she finally can move on.

Perdita's phone vibrates with a text message from her stepmom.

Almost done in there, honey?

Almost, Perdita lies, annoyed for the millionth time that she's still a year away from being old enough to get her driver's license.

Remember that we need to leave soon to pick up your sister.

Yeah. I know. Be out in a couple minutes.

Perdita slips her phone into her back pocket, hops the counter, and pushes through the unlocked door behind the register.

. . . .

FADE IN:

INT. CONTROL ROOM—NIGHT

BIG BRAIN is seated in the center of the room atop his floating throne surrounded by the blinking lights of the control panels that encircle him. His eyes are closed as if in meditation as his skull glows a calming white. A DOOR WHOOSHES OPEN off-screen, and FOOTSTEPS APPROACH. BIG BRAIN opens his eyes and smirks as WHITE SAVIOR walks toward him. Fresh out of the shower, her wet blond hair is combed back and she's changed into jeans and a T-shirt. She's carrying her crumpled, bloodstained White Savior suit, but when she reaches BIG BRAIN, she tosses it at his feet. His eyes go from the suit to White Savior.

BIG BRAIN

You're certain you do not wish to extend your contract
once more?

WHITE SAVIOR

For the last time: I'm sure.

BIG BRAIN

[Sighs] Of all my partners over the years, you were the most dynamic. Your performance in this final round alone! And the banter between us—[Chef's kiss gesture]

WHITE SAVIOR

We're *foes*, not "partners."

BIG BRAIN

If you insist.

BIG BRAIN's hovering throne lowers. He rises.

BIG BRAIN

But is it so easy to give up such power? Such wealth? Such renown?

WHITE SAVIOR

Let's skip to the part where you send me home.

BIG BRAIN

If you no longer care for the material benefits, then what about the people of the Third World you've sworn to protect? Surely you've some

sentiment for those you've been working to save so
diligently all these years? Is it so easy to turn your
back on them, to turn your back on being their hero?
Think of all the lives you have saved—could continue
to save.

WHITE SAVIOR

Think about all the lives *you* could save simply by not
being a homicidal megalomaniac.

BIG BRAIN

You have your role, I have mine. And we have
complemented each other so very well. Hence,
I am genuinely curious about your insistence
on ending our arrangement. What, pray tell, has
changed?

There's a long silence. WHITE SAVIOR walks to the windows, crosses
her arms, and gazes out at the stars. BIG BRAIN moves next to her. The
camera lingers on their reflections floating like apparitions over the
galaxy.

WHITE SAVIOR

For the first several years, I thought I was making a
difference . . . I thought I was changing the Third World
for the better.

BIG BRAIN

And then?

WHITE SAVIOR

And then I realized I'm not. No matter what I do, how
many people I save, it's never enough . . . I'm tired . . .
The Third World . . . it's a lost cause.

BIG BRAIN

Ah, don't think of it like that.

WHITE SAVIOR

How should I think of it?

BIG BRAIN

As our playing field.

WHITE SAVIOR

Then I guess you can say I'm done with the game. It's
time for me to go home.

BIG BRAIN

Hmm. If boredom is the issue, then perhaps we can
mix things up.

WHITE SAVIOR turns away from the window to face BIG BRAIN.

WHITE SAVIOR

What do you mean?

BIG BRAIN

I wasn't always Big Brain, you know.

WHITE SAVIOR

You weren't?

BIG BRAIN

Long ago, before wielding this formidable intellectual power, I actually wore the same suit as you.

WHITE SAVIOR

You're saying that *you* were White Savior?

BIG BRAIN

Indeed. I was once the protector of the Third World—which, back then, we called the Colonies—while another served as Big Brain.

WHITE SAVIOR

So what happened?

BIG BRAIN

[Begins to pace] After some time, I came to develop the same sense of hopelessness as you just now described. After all the work we had done to civilize those people, all the natural resources from which we had unburdened them, all the borders we had so carefully crafted. Except instead of quitting . . . I killed Big Brain. Foolishly, I believed that doing so would end the Colonies' persistent suffering once and for all.

WHITE SAVIOR

But it didn't.

BIG BRAIN

[Stops pacing] Obviously. As he died, something in the universe shifted. His power flowed into me, replacing my enhanced physical prowess with an enhanced mind. And I *became* him.

WHITE SAVIOR

You said you killed him because you wanted to end the suffering—so why didn't you use your powers as Big Brain to effect positive change throughout the Third World?

BIG BRAIN

With my newfound intellect, I instantly understood that just as every creature has its niche within an ecosystem, there have always been and will always be certain roles humanity requires. If there is to be a First World, there must be a Third World. If there is to be a Big Brain, then there must be a White Savior . . . That, and I realized the true causes of widespread systemic injustice and inequality were far too complex, too entangled, too numerous for me to solve without sacrificing the First World.

WHITE SAVIOR

And now you're proposing I kill you in order to "mix things up"?

BIG BRAIN

[Smirks] I propose that you *try*.

WHITE SAVIOR clenches her fists . . . then turns back to the window and unclenches them. She takes a deep breath, lets out a long, slow exhale, and falls quiet for a long time.

WHITE SAVIOR

No. I'm tired. I'm done. Take my powers back, and send me home.

BIG BRAIN

A shame. But a deal is a deal. You have survived another term. You no longer wish to renew. So I shall reunite you with your daughter.

BIG BRAIN steps uncomfortably close to WHITE SAVIOR and places his hands on her shoulders. WHITE SAVIOR winces at his touch but allows it. She closes her eyes and takes another deep breath as BIG BRAIN's skull begins to glow, cycling between red, white, and blue.

BIG BRAIN

This might tickle a bit.

BIG BRAIN closes his eyes. The glow of his oversized pulsating brain intensifies and accelerates. The light travels down his neck, through his arms, to his hands. After a few moments, WHITE SAVIOR's entire body begins to glow as well. Her jaw clenches and eyes shut even tighter as if in immense pain. Soon, the light burns a blinding white. Then, WHITE SAVIOR's body dims. The light travels back through BIG BRAIN's hands, arms, shoulders, and neck, until only his big brain glows white. Slowly, he opens his eyes and grins.

BIG BRAIN

It's done. Your powers are gone.

WHITE SAVIOR opens her eyes, which are now brown. She takes a deep breath. Blinks a few times. Looks at her hands and notices that her skin's a shade darker. Sensing that the burden of her powers has been lifted, a mixture of regret and relief passes over her face. Then she looks up. Looks around. Confusion and anger arrive as her gaze falls on BIG BRAIN.

WHITE SAVIOR

Why am I still in your godforsaken universe?

BIG BRAIN takes his time returning to his seat.

BIG BRAIN

Because interstitial travel is a one-way trip, my dear.
Once you leave a universe, there is no returning to that

universe. One of the few physical laws my formidable intellect has not yet found a way to alter.

WHITE SAVIOR rushes up to BIG BRAIN and grabs him violently by his dramatically high collar.

WHITE SAVIOR

You lied to me—you said you'd send me home to *my* universe—to my *daughter*!

BIG BRAIN

No, I said I'd *reunite* you with her. And if you would be so kind as to release me, that's exactly what I'll do.

WHITE SAVIOR

If this is some kind of trick, I'll—

BIG BRAIN

You'll what? No more powers, remember?

WHITE SAVIOR hesitates. Realizing he could easily kill her, she releases him.

BIG BRAIN fixes his collar. He repositions himself, takes a deep breath, closes his eyes, and touches his temples. His glowing brain begins to pulse once more, again cycling between red, white, and blue with increasing rapidity until there's a blindingly bright flash and then—

CUT TO: WHITE

[Sfx: DOORS WHOOSH OPEN. Hesitantly, FOOTSTEPS APPROACH.
Then stop.]

FADE IN:

INT. DOORWAY—NIGHT

A teenage girl with light brown skin, long black hair, and brown eyes
behind thick glasses stands a few steps past the threshold. This is
PERDITA PADILLA. She is looking around, disoriented—until her gaze
lands on JENNIFER DE LUCA (NÉE WHITE SAVIOR). Her eyes widen.
Her mouth stretches into a smile, a ship arriving home.

PERDITA PADILLA

Mom?

CUT TO: BLACK

. . . .

"Mom?" Perdita says.

Before Jennifer de Luca can respond, Perdita rushes over and
throws her arms around her mother.

"Mom," she says again, no longer a question. She cries and holds
this person she thought she would never hold again, determined to
never let go. Perdita is so lost in the moment that she does not notice
Jennifer is quiet, rigid, hesitant.

"How precious," says a man's voice nearby, breaking the spell.

Perdita finally pulls back from the hug and registers the supervillain's presence. "Big Brain?"

The man tips an imaginary hat.

Perdita blinks. Notices her mom's stunned silence and look of bewilderment. Takes in the control panels, the throne, the void outside the windows, the blood and guts splattered across the doorway. As she reorients herself, disorientation returns. "Wait—I'm . . . I'm on set?" She glances all around. "I've never seen this episode or read a script of anything like this." Her eyes widen. "It's the finale, isn't it?" She continues to look around. "But where are all the cameras?"

Jennifer steps back. She looks past Perdita. "What the hell is this, Big Brain?"

"Your daughter. As promised."

"My daughter was three when you took me away from her."

Perdita's smile falters. "Wait—what? What do you mean?"

"Yes, and she has grown up," Big Brain says, ignoring Perdita.

Jennifer steps forward, fists clenched. "You f—"

"Time does not translate across universes in predictable ways," Big Brain says as he makes a dismissive gesture and returns to his throne. He leans back in the seat. "Be grateful I am not only letting you live but that I have gone through the trouble of returning her to you at all."

"Mom, why's he talking as if all of this is real?" Perdita asks.

Jennifer hesitates, glaring at Big Brain. But after a moment, her fists unclench, and she shifts her attention to her daughter.

Her daughter.

Not as expected, but here, nonetheless. Just as she had to adjust to the reality of this universe after Big Brain plucked her from her own so many years ago, she will adjust to this. Her soul softens as she resigns herself to the imperfect solution.

"Perdita," she says, taking the girl's hand with a gentleness she couldn't initially summon. "This isn't a television studio. All of this— this world—isn't a show."

Perdita looks from her mother to Big Brain to her mother again. "Then I'm dreaming? Or hallucinating?"

"It's real."

Perdita is silent. She had always had the feeling *White Savior* was more than just television. That unnamed feeling drove her obsession, her search for the finale script to provide closure, to figure out what happened to her mom.

"Simply put, there are an infinite number of universes," Big Brain explains, "and I have figured out how to move individuals across them. Interstitial travel transforms beings into perfect vessels of energy. I can then imbue these vessels with abilities so that they may provide me with some measure of challenge."

"And why would you do that?" Perdita asks. "If you're so powerful, why do you need to . . . create opposition? Couldn't you just rule this universe without all the extra steps?"

"It's not about ruling the universe," Big Brain says. "Besides, that would be rather dull."

"So you stole my mom . . . for entertainment?"

"A crude sentiment, but yes. I suppose so."

Perdita rubs her face. "But back in my universe, you're characters in an old TV show. I've seen every episode. I own all the merchandise. I've read all—or almost all—the scripts. How is it that the writers knew all about *this* universe?"

"Few individuals are powerful enough to manipulate these universes as I can," Big Brain says, "but it's a common occurrence for some— dreamers, artists, prophets, and so on—to subconsciously glimpse other universes while not understanding that they are doing so. To put it simply, they believe they are creating while they are actually plagiarizing."

Perdita turns to Jennifer. "This doesn't make any fucking sense."

"I know. But it's true, honey. And it's all over." Jennifer squeezes her daughter's hand. "For me, anyway—I've completed my contracted term as White Savior. That's why you're here. I've given up my powers, and now I'm free to live my life—with you back in it."

Jennifer moves to hug Perdita again, but Perdita pulls away. Her face pinches with confusion as she struggles to grasp the implications, to untangle the reality from the performance. "Wait—it was just a job? You never really cared about the Third World?"

"At first, sure. But, eventually, I don't know . . . it was just so . . . exhausting." Jennifer runs her hands over her face. "I'm a good person. But it's complicated, okay?"

"So who's going to help all those people now?"

Jennifer glances at Big Brain, who shrugs. "Someone else," she says. "I've done what I can."

Perdita considers this for a long time. She doesn't like the idea of all those vulnerable people left without a savior, but she tries to accept that it's her mother's choice. And, selfishly, she's glad that her mother *chose* her. "Okay," she finally says. "Can we go home now?"

Jennifer shakes her head. "Sorry, but we can't."

Perdita's heart drops. "Wait—what? Why?"

After Big Brain explains the limits of interstitial travel, Perdita asks, "So we're stuck here?"

He nods.

She walks over to the window and gazes at the blue-and-green marbled orb below. Earth. But not *her* Earth. She thinks of her stepmother waiting in the car outside the store, her little sister waiting to be picked up from dance, her father cooking dinner at home.

"What happened to me back in my universe?" she asks. "Did I disappear like you did?"

"I suppose so," Jennifer says.

Perdita blinks back tears. Isn't this what she's always wanted—to find out what happened to her mom? To *find* her mom? But is it worth all the pain that will ripple in the wake of her absence from her home universe, all the suffering that will resonate throughout the Third World in the wake of White Savior's absence from this one?

"I need a minute," Perdita says, and walks away from the control center toward the exit. If her mother calls after her, she does not hear it.

Maybe, Perdita thinks, once she passes through the doors, she will find herself back in the collectibles store. She will climb into her annoying but well-meaning stepmother's car. They will pick up her sister from dance class and eat dinner with her father at home. Tomorrow, whatever all this was will be behind her, and she will sell her *White Savior* merchandise and never watch another episode so long as she lives.

Except that is not what happens. When the doors slide open, they reveal a hallway splattered with the blood and guts of Little Brown Brother #4. As Perdita crosses the threshold, the doors close behind her.

Alone amidst the gore, the truth of her new reality hits. The guilt.

It's too much for Perdita. She leans against the wall. Slides down to the floor. Drops her face into her hands and lets herself cry at the tangle of emotions swirling within her soul. There is no way out. No way to recover all she's lost.

Perdita cries until her throat hurts and her heart feels like an empty well. Except it's not empty—in the darkness at the bottom, something shiny: an idea.

Perdita sits up, clears her throat, and dries her eyes. She scans what remains of her mother's disposable sidekick until she spots what she's looking for gripped by the fist of a severed arm. She peels back the fingers, picks it up, and wipes it off.

One of Little Brown Brother's laser escrima sticks.

There's a heft to it she wasn't expecting, but it's otherwise identical to the replicas she owns in her home universe. She stands, tucks the weapon into the back of her pants, and returns to the control room.

If she's responsible for the fact that this world will no longer have White Savior, the least she can do is make sure it will also be free of Big Brain.

"Perdita!" Jennifer says, standing next to her erstwhile nemesis, face lighting up at the sight of her daughter.

"I told you she'd be back," Big Brain says. "Adolescence is such a volatile time."

Jennifer ignores him. "You'll get used to it here, I promise."

Perdita nods, approaching the pair with determined steps. "I know."

Her mother opens her arms once more—but Perdita ducks beneath them, ignites the laser escrima stick, and swings it at Big Brain's head.

The weapon halts a hairsbreadth away from his now-glowing skull as time seems to suddenly stop. Frozen midswing, Perdita can't move a single muscle but burns with the awareness of her failure.

"Whoa," Big Brain says, shifting to eye the laser-enhanced bamboo pole that nearly ended him. "That was close."

Big Brain blinks, and his oversized glowing head turns from white to red. Instantly, Perdita collapses to the ground and begins to scream and writhe in pain as she drops the escrima stick and it rolls away.

"BB, stop!" Jennifer pleads.

But Big Brain ignores her, lost in the pleasure of inflicting pain.

"Please!" Jennifer cries.

He continues to ignore her.

Without thinking, Jennifer picks up the escrima stick and slices through Big Brain's skull. His eyes widen in shock, then go vacant as the top half of his head slides away and plops onto the floor like a chunk of SPAM. A beat later, his body collapses—and then the two halves of his brain begin sputtering and sparking, twitching and flashing as if short-circuiting. Each erratic burst of energy jolts the room, as if the whole world is glitching.

Jennifer goes to Perdita's side, eyes wide with panic. "Are you okay?"

Perdita rolls over, groaning.

Jennifer lets out a relieved exhale. She brushes a stray strand of her daughter's hair behind her ear. "I'm sorry."

Perdita slowly opens her eyes. "Wait—why?"

A blinding white light fills the room.

· · · · · · · · · · · ·

CUT TO:

EXT. COLLECTIBLES SHOP—DAY

PERDITA PADILLA, an obsessive teenage fan of the *White Savior* TV series, stands at the cash register of BB's Vintage Toy Dungeon, Los Angeles. She is clutching a bound script in her hands. The SHOP-KEEPER, a balding elder millennial in a *Quantum Leap* T-shirt, watches with growing impatience.

SHOPKEEPER

So, you going to buy it, or what?

PERDITA

[Glances around, puzzled] Sorry—spaced out there for a moment. Um . . . can you tell me where I am?

SHOPKEEPER

Um . . . Are you okay?

PERDITA

Please, just tell me where I am.

SHOPKEEPER

You're in a store. Buying that. [Gestures to the bound pages in Perdita's hands]

PERDITA

[Looks down, skims the first page and gasps, then flips through the rest of the pages and looks up] This is the script for the finale episode?

SHOPKEEPER

For real, you okay?

PERDITA

Yes or no?

SHOPKEEPER

Yeah, yeah. *White Savior*'s last episode.

PERDITA

It *was* just a dream.

SHOPKEEPER

Um . . . what?

PERDITA

. . . Nothing. How much do I owe you?

SHOPKEEPER

A Tubman.

PERDITA

Huh?

SHOPKEEPER

A ten.

PERDITA

Ten dollars—that's it?

SHOPKEEPER

Yeah. I mean, not much demand. It was a notoriously
terrible episode.

PERDITA

Wait—you've seen it?

SHOPKEEPER

Who hasn't? All those ridiculous plot twists that came
out of nowhere ruined an otherwise amazing series.
The definition of failing to stick the landing.

PERDITA

Oh. Right.

PERDITA digs through her bag for a ten-dollar bill. Finding one, she
examines the picture of Harriet Tubman for a confused moment before
handing it to the SHOPKEEPER. The SHOPKEEPER rings up the sale
and slides the script back across the counter. PERDITA picks it up, flipping through the pages as she exits.

CUT TO:

EXT. PARKING LOT—DAY

In the parking lot, a WOMAN is waiting in a car. It is PERDITA'S STEPMOM.

STEPMOM

Ready to go, Perdita?

PERDITA

[Looks up, smiles] Yeah. I am.

STEPMOM

Great! Your sister is—

The car explodes, shattering storefront windows and knocking PER-
DITA back. Her body is still as the car burns, dust clouds the parking

lot, and debris flutters from the sky. Eventually, PERDITA climbs slowly to her feet. Realizing what's happened, panic sets in. She rushes toward the car but stops short of the flames and shouts for someone to help.

A FIGURE appears. Their identity is obscured by the smoke—except for a dim glow where the FIGURE's head should be. Slowly, they approach. PERDITA does not notice at first, but then she looks up. Recognition sparks in her eyes.

PERDITA

Big Brain . . .

MYSTERIOUS FIGURE

In a way . . .

The FIGURE steps through the smoke. It is a white woman with brown eyes and blond hair tied up into a tight bun. She has an oversized head that's pulsing with a red glow and is wearing an ostentatious supervillain outfit with a dramatically high collar. In one hand, she carries a box.

PERDITA

Mom?

PERDITA'S MOTHER/MYSTERIOUS FIGURE

I'm sorry, honey—I had to kill Big Brain to save you. But because I did so, the universe made me become what he was.

PERDITA

And did the universe also make you kill my
stepmother?

PERDITA'S MOTHER/MYSTERIOUS FIGURE/BIG BRAIN

. . . I need you to hate me.

PERDITA

Why?

Fire still smoldering, dust and debris still hanging in the air, PERDITA'S
MOTHER steps up to PERDITA and hands her the box. Reluctantly,
PERDITA opens the lid, pauses, and pulls out its contents. Shaking her
head, PERDITA holds it up. In the flickering light of the flames, we see
it is the WHITE SAVIOR suit.

PERDITA'S MOTHER/MYSTERIOUS FIGURE/BIG BRAIN

Because I need you to become White Savior. As
someone who's traveled across universes, you're
the only person in this world I can imbue with the
powers—at least for now.

PERDITA

But I'm only half white.

PERDITA'S MOTHER/MYSTERIOUS FIGURE/BIG BRAIN

It's more of a mindset.

PERDITA

[Looking up] And if I refuse?

PERDITA'S MOTHER/MYSTERIOUS FIGURE/BIG BRAIN

Then who will save the Global South?

PERDITA turns away from her MOTHER and toward the flaming wreckage of her stepmother's car. Her soul is so conflicted, it feels as if it will tear asunder. She does not want to become her mother's archnemesis. But if she does not step up, who will save the Global South?

On second thought, maybe the people of the Global South could figure things out for themselves—especially if Big Brain and White Savior weren't constantly intervening in their lives. Maybe what they needed wasn't an epic ongoing battle between good and evil but reparations and the cessation of exploitation by the Global North.

Eh, but it would be cool to be a hero.

PERDITA

Fine.

CUT TO: BLACK

CUE CREDITS AND CLOSING THEME SONG

Take It from Me
by David Levithan

It started with a spoon.

I was six, maybe seven. Old enough to know right from wrong, but young enough that deciding between the two always felt situational, spontaneous. We were over at my great-aunt Agnes's apartment—an apartment as antiquated as her name. Plenty of candlesticks, each with a lace doily at its base. Wooden bookshelves crowding the walls, the books untouched, nearly forlorn. The only wall without a shelf was adorned by a filmy mirror, a strange drawing of a dancing monkey, and—pride of place, right in the middle—a display rack of souvenir spoons.

I was utterly fascinated by these spoons, especially because they had *never actually been used as spoons*. They were not for cereal, not for soup. They were collectibles, curiosities, each with a distinctive identity embedded in its handle. It is possible that this spoon collection did more for my knowledge of geography than any other tool, because I was fascinated by the distinction between the sunset mountains commemorated on the Utah spoon and the vast canyon on the Arizona spoon and the winking hula dancer on . . . well, you know which spoon that was, don't you? The miraculous thing was that Aunt Agnes had collected them all herself—miraculous because I had never seen Agnes outside her apartment, couldn't imagine her visiting my own house in a nearby suburb, let alone discovering a spoon in the far-off wilds of Denmark. In my head, I formed it into a fantasy story, a grand quest. To break a curse, she'd had to travel to all these lands and capture every single one of these spoons. I regarded them with a reverence that not even Agnes seemed to possess.

I was told in no uncertain terms that the spoons were *not toys*, and I was not meant to touch them, in the same way I was not meant to touch the old rifles my grandfather kept mounted on *his* walls. My mother in particular could see me eyeing them and tried to distract me with coloring books and Matchbox cars. This worked . . . for a time. Visit after visit, my attention would wander to the rack. Each spoon was gripped by the neck, but held loosely. Some leaned over; some leaned in. I imagined they were waving to me. When no one else was looking, I waved back.

Our visits couldn't have been long, nor could there have been that many of them. Aunt Agnes was kin, but not our responsibility. Sometimes my grandfather came along; sometimes it was just Mom, Dad, and me. I don't remember very much about the visits, although there have been times when I've walked into rooms and been struck by a scent distinctly similar to the olifactory underpinnings of Aunt Agnes's place. Hint of wilted flowers and talcum. Shadowy smell of wet birch. False forest of the bathroom cleaner.

I don't remember much, but I remember my first theft. I don't know why I was left alone in the room, only that I had to have been alone. When I stood, I could reach only the lowest row of spoons. On close examination, I realized that the rings around their necks weren't solid—there were gaps in the backs, to make it easier to put them into place. This was not a permanent installation. The spoons were . . . removable.

This is where it gets interesting, at least to me. There were some spoons in that bottom row that dazzled me: the one with the Eiffel Tower as its handle; the one with the small gondola and the even smaller gondolier; the one with a tail shaped like a heart, with (mysterious!) no discernible location attached. Common heist logic followed that I would choose the spoon I found most valuable, or at least the one I loved the most. But instead, as I set about to do something I sensed was inherently wrong (i.e., stealing), I followed my own heist logic, and tried, in as little time as possible, to discern which of the spoons was the least valuable, the least interesting, the least likely to be missed. It was not a spoon from a foreign land or a spoon of an enticing shape that I took down from its perch and placed in my pocket. Instead, it was a spoon from the Empire State Building—a building that, were there not other buildings in the way, could have been seen from Aunt Agnes's window.

I didn't lose my cool. Not when an adult inevitably came back into the room. Not when I got back home and had to take the spoon out of my pocket before my pants went into the hamper. For a hiding place, I chose the box of a puzzle I knew had missing pieces, a puzzle that no one was going to ever ask me to put together again. I put the spoon inside and rarely took it out. It was enough to know it was there.

If Aunt Agnes ever missed it, I never knew. I remember going back to that apartment and seeing the empty space, but I was the only person who seemed to notice the gap. Eventually, she sold the apartment and moved to Florida. I don't know what happened to the spoons.

What I do know is this: I had started my first and only collection.

As a child, I loved to draw maps of imaginary places. I loved to name different areas in my backyard and map those too. There was a methodology to which stuffed animals slept in my bed and which slept under the bed. I liked to rotate the cereal I had for breakfast, so that a Cheerios day always followed a Frosted Flakes day. I kept track of my video game scores, and sometimes would set up brackets where I would play against myself using different alter egos, a self-serious Olympics.

In other words, I loved rules and systems—as long as I was in control of them. My imagination was the place where I had the most power. Hour after hour, I was asked to conform to the world, and as a result I searched out all the small ways I could make the world conform to me.

My cousin Alanna collected shells. She didn't tell me this, but collections are easy to spot when you know to look for them. They are never in a place of immediate need; very rarely do people keep their collections on the nightstands next to their beds, or on the same dressers where they put their house keys. Often they reside in the least traveled spot in the room, or (for adults) the least traveled room in the house. In the case of Alanna's shells, they filled a fishbowl unceremoniously plunked on a shelf otherwise devoted to her least-worn sweaters. I only knew it was a collection because I'd been with her on beach vacations, where her mother would bring back shells from her walks and say, "Look what I found for your collection." Alanna would look up from her phone, and would sometimes even say thank you. But I never saw her search for shells herself.

This made it an easy, ultimately unsatisfying theft. I realized I had a new condition for my own collection; in order for me to steal something valuable, it would have to be valued. It also had to be seen as a collection; my mother, for example, had a lot of earrings, but I don't think she ever would have said she had an earring collection. I realized the less functional an item, the more likely it was to be a part of a collection.

Second grade. Third grade. Fourth grade. I tried to get myself invited over to friends' houses as often as I could, because while kids sometimes brought samples of their collections for show-and-tell, it was too hard to steal from them in school. Dominic kept his baseball cards in plastic sleeves; I asked my dad who the least valuable player would be, then drafted him the first time Dominic left him unprotected. Miranda was partial to pony figurines; I asked her if we could play with them, then noticed which ones she left in the stable. Braden was a fanatical connoisseur of all things Pokémon. He kept offering to trade me cards, and when I told him I didn't have any, he started pestering me to buy some packs so we could trade. He had four Charmanders, so I figured he wouldn't miss one. I ended up being wrong, but luckily had placed it in my sock, not my pockets, because he made me empty my pockets in front of him. Our friendship struggled after that.

I started to catalog the sources of my trove, writing them on the backs of puzzle pieces. The weird thing was, I didn't need much help in remembering. Laura Miller left our school in fourth grade, but years later, after everyone else had forgotten she'd ever been there, her name would come immediately to mind when I held the four-leaf clover charm that had dropped off her bracelet during recess, my own little piece of luck.

In sixth grade I became friends with Dylan Coopersmith. He had a very specific collection of banana stickers. Not stickers that showed bananas, but the stickers that appeared on bananas. He didn't have to have eaten the banana himself; apparently, friends and family members kept hold of their banana stickers to hand over the next time they saw him. One whole wall of his bedroom was covered in these stickers, and the problem (for me) was that he kept count of every single one. In fact, as I learned on a sleepover, when he was too anxious to go to sleep, he would count them until he was calm enough to slumber.

It meant so much to him that it meant a lot to me to get a sticker for myself. As if to insulate myself from the guilt of my theft-to-be, I became one of his suppliers. I didn't even like bananas, but I asked my mom to get some and would dutifully introduce them into my morning cereal just so I could get the sticker off the peel. (In explaining his collection to me, Dylan had made it very clear that it was against the rules to simply remove the stickers from the bananas while they were perched for adoption at the supermarket. The only valid sticker was a genuinely owned sticker.)

I had never thought of banana stickers as having remarkable adhesive quality. But I swear, when no one else was around, Dylan must have ironed those stickers onto the wall, because every time I came over, I couldn't find a single dangling edge. Even the stickers I brought him were immediately pressed into place with a religious fervor. Then he entered the new tally (1434!) into his notebook.

The big problem was that when I was over, Dylan never left me alone in his room. From what I could tell, showers weren't his thing. If I expressed hunger, he would call to his mom that we were hungry, and she would deliver a snack (or tell both of us to get down to the kitchen). I couldn't even get a moment when he was in the bathroom, because his bathroom was attached to his room, and he was so silent when he peed that I could imagine him hearing every step I made.

I started to resent Dylan. He was one of those friends who, when he invited you over, became King of His Room. I was more his subject than his guest; it was always *let's play this* and *let's play that*. If I'd wanted my free will imposed upon, I could have just stayed at home.

Finally, an opportunity arose. We were playing a board game

that he was good at (he only chose board games he was good at), and when he did a little victory jump after defeating my army, he knocked over the glass of juice his mother had delivered a short time before. For a second, he stared at the resulting puddle as if someone else was going to deal with it. Then, seeing that I was making no move, he sprang to his feet and said he'd be right back; he had to get some paper towels. I sprang up too, and when he left for the kitchen, I went straight to the wall. After perilous seconds of searching, I was gifted with the sight of a sticker with a corner tabbing slightly out, the most subtle come-hither.

I pulled. The bottom of the sticker lifted; the top clung. The word CHIQUITA was mine. Chiquita's elbow was mine. I could hear Dylan pounding up the stairs. I pulled at the top of her dress—too much, too fast. Her head clung to the wall, and the rest of her ripped off between my thumb and my forefinger. I barely had time to put my hand in my pocket when Dylan came in with a whole roll of paper towels and then, to my utter astonishment, proceeded to wheel it over the puddle as if it were a rolling pin. The juice was quickly sopped up, but the roll was rendered worthless.

I got the ¾ sticker off my fingers and onto the lining of my pocket. Dylan didn't sense anything was wrong, and I didn't feel I'd done anything particularly wrong . . . not until I was home and putting the ¾ sticker into the puzzle box, stuck to the back of a puzzle piece with a little dangling off, just in case I had to move it later on. That should have been that. But later, when I was trying to fall asleep, I kept thinking of the way Dylan would chirp his tally (1442!) and how I was the only one who'd know that he was actually (1441 ¼!) now off. In other words, it no longer felt like a victimless crime, and that manifested in my mind as anguish.

There was only one way to remedy this. The next day, I surreptitiously ate four bananas, just so my mother would have to buy more. Once she did, I procured the sticker and, with the eye of a master forger, ripped it in (roughly) the same place as the one I'd taken. Then I had to get myself invited back over to Dylan's house. The only way to do this was to appeal to the king himself, to tell him how much I missed his kingdom. I must have been pretty convincing, because he invited me over that very afternoon. I called my mother to tell her. He didn't bother calling his mother to warn her.

Once we got to his room and he set up the same game as last time, I looked for my moment. I contemplated asking for juice just so I could knock it over. I wondered what he would do if I told him I smelled smoke. Finally, nature helped me out, because he told me he had to go to the bathroom. Unfortunately, he decided to leave the door open while he peed because, I realized, he was afraid I would cheat at the board game he was otherwise going to win. There was enough of a blind spot, though, for me to stand up and get to the spot with the sticker I'd beheaded. It took a moment to find . . . but then I located it . . . took out my replacement ¾ . . . reached up . . .

"What are you doing?"

I froze, the sticker stuck in its trajectory inches from the wall. Then I turned to see Dylan in the doorway of his bathroom, fly still unzipped, staring at me.

"It fell off," I said. "I'm putting it back."

"What?"

I watched as he undoubtedly cycled through all the other explanations for what I was doing, trying to find a more probable one than the one I'd offered. Then, not finding one, he came over to me and said, "Give me that."

For two sixth-grade boys, we effected a very delicate transfer, as if the banana sticker were a dried butterfly wing. When I pointed out the space where it needed to go, Dylan huffed, *"I know."* I didn't look too closely, but I didn't think he'd managed to get the two pieces evenly lined. Chiquita would always bear the scars of my deception.

We didn't speak of the sticker again. Instead, we sat back down on the floor, and Dylan beat me three arduous times in a row. Only three things made this bearable: my relief at covering up my theft; the fact that I knew I'd never have to go over to Dylan's house again; and the simple, petty truth that every time he gloated, I could think, *Your fly is open and you still haven't noticed.*

I am a reliable narrator, but I shouldn't necessarily be considered a sympathetic one.

Is it hormonal, the way that most kids get to a certain age and don't bother with collections anymore? It's a benign neglect—I don't think many kids actually proclaim, *I am done with collections; collections are for babies!* the way they do with, say, dolls or training wheels. But when the time comes for a room makeover, the collections are among the first things to be sent to the reliquary in the basement or, if storage is tight, eternal rest in the nearest landfill. The majority of teens let go of whatever they once gathered, because the gathering was nominal, almost obligatory. And the minority who keep hold? Well, they keep hold hard, because the gathering runs deep.

I was not a teen who collected friends, who wanted my birthday party to be the event of the season. The fact that I was friends with a lot of kids seemed almost accidental; I had an O-negative personality. I had inadvertently fashioned myself into someone who wasn't a confessor or a competitor, but was always a good person to have around. I didn't do this in order to gain access to their lives or their collections . . . but I didn't balk when opportunities arose to suss out those friends who still collected, and to take a piece of whatever they'd gathered.

It would be a mistake to think the collectors were always the outcasts or the misfits, substituting decorative thimbles for social interactions. In ninth grade, Antonio Perch, junior varsity quarterback, was obsessive about his coin collection—the concept being that money you never spent would someday be worth much more than its face value. (I substituted my own Iowa state quarter for his Iowa state quarter, so I wouldn't compromise his completism.) Saundra Diaz, who at least seven people of various genders wanted to ask to the homecoming dance, had never smoked a cigarette in her life, but she'd inherited an ashtray collection from her grandmother, and felt it her filial duty to continue, even if ashtrays were harder and harder to come by. (Even though it was a large item for me, I took one from the "annex" of undisplayed ashtrays, from a golf tournament in 1978.)

And then there was Hannah Coors, my first truly kleptomaniac friend. On the surface level, you would think we had a lot in common—i.e., she liked to steal, and I liked to steal. But it was one of those situations where our handling of the thing in common actually spelled out how deeply apart we were. I prided myself in the focus of my thefts—I had laid down a certain set of criteria, and every theft needed to clear the threshold of those criteria. Hannah, on the other hand, grabbed whatever the fuck she wanted. Possibly she introduced the criterion of whether or not she'd get caught; often, I felt this criterion was blurry at best, disregarded at worst. I don't say this as a joke—Hannah's kleptomania did appear to my teenage self to be an actual mania, and I didn't have the vocabulary to deal with that. She never stole from me, but she stole wherever we went. CVS. Movie theater. The Gap. The car wash. I was perpetually terrified we'd get caught, while she seemed perpetually thrilled.

Some of her trove was regifted, a strange Robin Hood–ing of lip gloss and mittens, bags of M&M's and electric toothbrushes. But there were also items she kept for herself, a hall of fame of the five-finger discount. Some of these items were expensive—pilfered jewelry, electronics that required the circumvention of alarms. But others were more personal. A lot of cartoon cat figurines. Items with Fanta branding, because Hannah really liked Fanta. A few items from her namesake brand of beer.

It wasn't hard to get myself invited to her house; after each theft, she usually wanted to go straight home to unload what she'd pilfered. She clearly enjoyed me being part of the routine, more because of my role as witness than from any accomplicehood. She didn't think I had a thieving bone in my body. Which only made me want to steal from her more.

Unlike Dylan, Hannah didn't mind leaving me in her room for long stretches of time. So it was fairly easy for me to study her hoard and choose the right easily missable object: a ceramic basset hound, about the size of my thumb, who hovered in the back of her display, as if intimidated by the dominance of all the felines.

When she came back into the room, the hound was safe in my backpack. A few minutes later, she reached under her bed and pulled out a scarf she'd stolen for me from a very upscale store in the mall. Without doubt, the most expensive thing that's ever touched my neck. I thanked her, and she seemed to notice something was off. She mistook it for me feeling guilty that she had gotten me something so pricey, and by such dubious means.

"Mr. Burberry won't miss a thing," she assured me, and I wondered if it would play out the same with her.

I knew I'd taken a risk, since it wasn't like Hannah's room was a heavily trafficked area with plenty of suspects if she noticed the theft. And indeed, the next day she asked me if I'd happened to see a dog lying around her room when I'd been over.

"I thought you only collected cats," I said, with what I hoped was a catlike nonchalance.

"Mostly," she replied. Then she changed the subject.

Two days later, after stealing a pair of almond croissants from a local bakery (without, somehow, leaving a trail of sugar), Hannah asked if we could go over to my house instead of hers.

"Just for a change of pace," she said.

I panicked and immediately made an excuse. I told her my dad was working at home, and that there wasn't any privacy when he was there, because he liked to pace when he talked on the phone. That last part was true, but that was the only true part.

Hannah seemed to take it in stride.

"No worries," she said. "Next time."

She didn't say "next time" ominously, but that's how I heard it. I felt like she had to be planning something. A rescue mission for the basset hound. Or, worse, since I had breached the rules of nonaggression in our friendship, she would feel okay to steal whatever she liked from my room. Even the puzzle box of collected items, if she found it.

No, *when* she found it. I was convinced she would find it.

I tried to convince myself that "next time" was just something people said. But three days later, when we were out with a couple other friends, she suggested it again—*let's go over to your place.*

I made another excuse.

And again, the time after that.

She never called me on it, but she also didn't hide her disappointment. She stopped asking me along on her "excursions," and soon we weren't hanging out at all outside of school. Was it because she knew I'd stolen from her, or was it because she now thought I was afraid of her stealing from me? I stayed as far away from these questions as I could.

October of our junior year, she was caught taking a wet vac from Target. From what I heard, her parents were surprised. She told them it was the first time, and they believed her. She stayed away from Target, but a few weeks later, was caught at the mall. This time, the police were involved. She was sent away for help. I want to say she wasn't even given a chance to say goodbye, but she said goodbye to a lot of other people. Just not me.

By the time she got back, we barely nodded to each other in the halls. She found a new group of friends.

And me?

Well, by then I was in love.

They went by the name K. I'm not being mysterious here, or trying to protect their identity. They just liked the sound of K. I never asked what it stood for, if it stood for anything at all. That was none of my business.

It was a classic setup: They were new to our town, and I didn't notice them right away. Or I noticed them, but didn't register it right away. It was a big school, and we had lots of new kids every year. But K was in my English class, and the whole going-by-an-initial and the whole going-by-they/them got my attention. There weren't many of us they/thems in our high school. I'm sure each one of us took an occasional census on who the others were. I upped the number by one after that first English-class roll call. But it was probably another two weeks before we actually spoke.

Then, once we started, we couldn't stop.

I still don't know how to explain it. It was like we both got on a seesaw at the same time, and all the ups and downs were under our control, and we enjoyed them. It wasn't a contest. It was a collaboration. And there wasn't ever the fear that the other person would leap off and send you crashing with a hard thud.

What I'm trying to say is: We trusted each other. From the start. We understood that we didn't understand each other completely, but we understood each other more than most.

The "dating" I'd done up until that point had started sideways— either a friend would turn into someone I was dating, or there was a need for a pairing and I said sure when someone asked me to go to a dance, or out to the movies, or whatever. But with K it was different. I flat-out asked them on a date, and they flat-out said yes. We went to a museum together, then made out a little in the park afterward. "We are so ridiculous," we kept saying. But it wasn't a criticism. We were happy with each other, and we were happy with ourselves when we were together.

They came over to my house before I went over to theirs. Unlike how it would have been like with Hannah, I wasn't worried K would go searching in my closet. I'd added to the collection lately—a Christmas ornament here, a vintage Beanie Baby there—but nothing I felt like boasting about. Early on, I'd asked K if they had any collections, and they'd said, "Not really." I was fine with that. Relieved, even. It wasn't something that hovered as we got to know each other.

We'd been officially dating for about two months when I finally got to see their bedroom.

It was about half the size of my room, just a bed and some borderland. If we'd both stood with our arms outstretched, we could have held hands and touched the opposite walls at the same time. But the size wasn't the most important thing about K's room. No, what struck me most about it was how closely it resembled a nest. K had spent years gathering images and textures and colors, and then wove them onto the walls and across the shelves. Some of these objects had stories attached, which K was happy to share with me. Other objects were chosen for more aesthetic gleanings. The room wasn't a collection except in the loosest sense, that the objects within it had been collected. But there was no central theme; these were not variations on the same object, like spoons or banana stickers or antique Coke bottles.

Once I'd gotten the tour, we kissed a little, then ended up on the floor to do some homework. That's when I noticed the locked chest at the foot of their bed. It didn't call attention to itself; if anything, it looked like it was trying to retreat under the bedskirt. Its most distinguishing feature was its brass lock, the keyhole in that chess-bishop shape that few keyholes are anymore.

"What's that?" I asked.

"What's what?"

"The box. What's inside?"

There was a pause. Not a long pause, but still a noticeable pause. When you see someone you like weighing a decision, it creates a momentary suspense of the heart, and that's what I felt right then, as if my pulse had gotten caught up in K's silent deliberations. I was being tested, and I wanted to pass the test and be worthy of whatever answer K was contemplating.

Then—*there*—the moment of response, the crescendo of the interpersonal suspense.

"Doubts," K said simply. "That box is where I keep my doubts."

This wasn't sarcasm or banter. This wasn't evasion.

The box was where they kept their doubts.

"I must have started when I was nine or ten," K continued. "I was friends with this girl Delia. Or I wanted to be friends with her. Her birthday was coming up, and she made a really big deal about it. I just knew that I wasn't going to be included . . . but I didn't want to tell anyone else that. Especially not my parents, because it wasn't out of the question that they'd call Delia's parents. So instead I wrote it down on a piece of paper—*I will never be invited to Delia's party. I will never be invited to Delia's party.* Then I folded it up and put it in this box, which my Uncle Reggie had gotten me for my birthday. He owns a pawnshop and gives the strangest gifts. But the point is . . . I liked writing it down and putting it away. It made me think about it from a distance. So I kept doing it. When I had doubts about other people. Or myself. Or some combination of the two."

"And did Delia invite you to her party?"

"Nope. But these two other kids, Ramón and Tara, weren't invited either, and so I asked them if they wanted to have a sleepover that night, and we ended up having a much better time. Or at least that's how I choose to remember it."

"And you still put doubts in there?"

"Yep."

"Do you ever read them over?"

"Not often. Maybe if I'm putting one in, I'll pick another out to read it, just to give myself some perspective. Most of them seem silly once some time has passed. But I still like to have them. My collection of doubts."

K had no idea what their use of the word *collection* would do to me. I hadn't been thinking of the box in those terms . . . but once K called it a collection, I felt a different kind of pull toward it, something greater than mere curiosity.

I immediately knew the threat.

Don't ruin this, I told myself. I didn't ask anything else about the box. I went back to kissing and homework, homework and kissing.

Leave it alone, I instructed myself.

But even then, I wasn't sure it would leave me alone.

The timing wasn't good.

I was perilously close to exhausting the collections of the people I knew. I'd stolen from relatives, from friends. In order to keep my collection going, I needed one of two things to happen: either the relatives and friends I'd already stolen from had to start new collections, or I needed to find new people with collections of their own. But the thing is, once you have one collection, it's rare to start others. It happens; I'm sure there are people (mostly rich people) who have numerous collections. And there are hoarders, but hoarders didn't have the curatorial, focused eye that attracted me.

As for new friends . . . I found making friends on such a scale as to be invited to their homes and witness to their collections to be a lot of work. And at that time, I wanted to focus most of my time and energy on K, because K deserved it.

So what was I going to do? Start befriending fifth graders so I could take what I needed from them? Start volunteering in old-age homes to pick through the remnants of collections that had stood the test of time? Just the fact that I was thinking along these lines made me disgusted with myself. If I had criteria, I also had to have boundaries. And within those boundaries, there was a strange gray zone: K's collection of doubts.

I prided myself in being a sensible, undramatic teenager. But as the weekiversaries turned to monthiversaries, my feelings toward K started to undermine my sensibility and inflame my dramatic thoughts. When I saw them jotting something down on a piece of paper and folding it up, I wondered if it was a doubt . . . and, specifically, if it was a doubt about me. Sometimes they'd end up passing me these notes, to ask me something logistical during class, where phones were forbidden. But other times, the folded squares would end up in their book bag, and it would take a mighty bout of drama-negation for me to avoid seeking a moment to peek inside.

Another fundamental problem was that K and I felt most comfortable making out when we were at home, not subject to anyone else's possible comment. When we were at my house, I lived in fear that K would for some reason uncover my collection collection, which now resided in three different puzzle boxes. (I actually stocked extra boxes of real puzzles, just in case K said they wanted to do a puzzle.) And when we were at K's house, I was hyperconscious of the doubt box. I'd gone as far as checking to make sure that it was, indeed, locked. Then I spotted an old-fashioned key on K's key ring, and knew what it had to be.

I could pull it off. I was sure I could steal the key, open the box, go through the contents, and take a minor doubt away from K. I wasn't particularly afraid of being caught.

I just knew, more than I'd known before, it was wrong.

Knowing the things you shouldn't do, and then not doing them:

That's what love requires, doesn't it? Even as a junior in high school, I sensed this was true. Love was both closeness and an agreement to never take advantage of that closeness. Love was respecting the border between the secrets the other person would share and the secrets they wanted to keep.

If only love didn't also curse us with impulses that run contrary to what we know we should do.

One time I tried to talk to K about it, in an indirect fashion. We were walking to a coffee shop after school, planning to park ourselves on that neutral ground for a couple hours of studying and not-studying.

"I'm not sure we're going to get that much work done," K said. "Though I really need to."

"Is that going in your doubt box?" I asked lightly.

But something was off, either with me asking the question or the way K chose to react. Instead of making a joke, or asking me where the question had really come from, they flatly said, "No, that wouldn't qualify."

I should have left it there. But impulse swelled, and I found myself asking, "Do you ever put doubts about me in the doubt box?"

"I doubt myself all the time," K replied. "Why wouldn't you be eligible?"

"I'll take that as a yes."

"I don't think you should take it as anything."

"Okay . . ."

We'd arrived at the door to the coffee shop. We went to the counter and ordered our drinks. K repeated that we really had to get some work done. So we got some work done.

I didn't bring the doubt box up again.

But I kept thinking about it.

. . . .

I started to stare at the puzzle boxes at the bottom of my closet. I wouldn't open them, or even try to inventory their contents in my head.

K knew what their collection was for. But I was wondering about mine.

Three more times over the next month or two, I was in the presence of the box and the key.

Three more times, K left me alone in their room.

I knew there would be things written about me inside the box.

I knew there would be information about K I hadn't yet been told.

I knew there had to be a slip of paper in there that K would never miss.

But then I mocked myself: Did I really think that stealing something unmemorable wouldn't be a violation of K's trust?

What are you keeping from me? I wondered.

In love, that is always a trick question.

I am not dwelling here on everything that was working, the fact that what I had with K was a near-perfect first relationship. We were good companions on the arc of mutual education that must define all significant first relationships. I made them laugh a lot, and they made me laugh a lot—I say this even though neither one of us was a laugher, but instead we expressed our good humor in grins and headshakes and nods of appreciation. I could list all the songs we learned from each other by sharing headphones. I could accentuate the joy with which we sang along.

That's all a part of the story.

Another part of the story is this:

One day, almost a year into dating, we went up to K's room and the box was gone.

"What did you do with it?" I asked, and at first K had no idea what I meant. So I clarified: "The box with your doubts. The doubt collection. Where did it go?"

"It looked really ugly there, and I kept tripping on it. I also thought it was silly at this point to be putting doubts in a box when they can just as easily go in my journal."

"So after all those years of doing it, you can change it just like that?"

There was a beat as K studied my expression, and I became aware that it was perhaps a more passionate expression than would have been ordinarily required for such a conversation.

"Why do you care?" they asked.

"I don't know," I said. "It's just . . . it was your collection. If you just list doubts in your journal, it's not still a collection, is it?"

"I guess that depends on your definition of *collection*. And I'm sensing that you might have your own definition. Care to enlighten me?" K sat on the floor, right where the box had been.

I backed down. "No, it's okay. I guess I was used to the box being there, that's all." I lowered myself next to K, leaned against the bed.

K knew me well enough by then to know there was something I wasn't saying. At that moment, they asked me the one question that no one had asked before.

"Do you have a collection? Something like the box?"

My first instinct was to lie—but my second instinct was to realize that the first instinct was a defensive impulse, and K deserved better than a defensive impulse.

So I told them. The truth . . . but a qualified truth. I started off by saying, "When I was a kid, I liked to collect things from other people's collections." I told K about Aunt Agnes, about other cousins and school friends stolen from, ending with Dylan. I made it sound like an anecdote, not an active condition.

K leaned their head on my shoulder and put their hand on mine.

"That's such a kid thing to do," they said. "It's so sad."

"Sad?"

"Yeah. That you felt the need to ruin everyone else's fun just to have your own. There's enough of that going around with adults today. At least in kids it's excusable."

"You're right," I said, even as I could feel my younger self's outrage at my betrayal. *Nobody noticed!* they insisted. *Nobody cared!*

"Do you still have it?" K asked.

"No," I said. "Not really."

We left it at that.

When I got home that night, I emptied my collection onto my bed.

I had never done this before. I'd reached in and pulled things out at random, but I'd never looked at everything at once.

It was heartbreaking. What had once seemed like treasure now seemed like trinkets.

The ones that had a story attached, like Aunt Agnes's spoon or Dylan's banana sticker, made me feel something, even if the stories seemed less exciting now than they had at the time. Other objects belonged to forgotten people and forgotten thefts. Sometimes I'd read the name on the puzzle piece attached to the item and remember, oh yes, this was from that relative, or this was from that friend. Other times, the names barely rang a bell, or missed the bell entirely. Even as a junior in high school, I was forgetting people. Having a piece of their collection didn't make me any closer to them than I otherwise would have been.

I couldn't imagine ever showing this collection to K. I couldn't imagine showing it to anyone. I didn't take any satisfaction from it anymore. So why did it exist?

The simple reaction would have been to sweep all the objects off my bed into a garbage bag and mutter, "My childhood is over," a few dozen times as I took the bag to the curb. But that's not what happened. Instead, I separated the objects into three piles.

The first pile went back into one of the puzzle boxes, with Aunt Agnes's spoon going in first. Even if the collection didn't bring me satisfaction, it still meant something to me. I kept this portion of it for the same reason I'd told K about it—because it was a part of me now, whether I liked it or not.

The second pile went into the garbage. The more trivial items. The larger items. The items that belonged to the people who'd already left my life.

The third pile required some follow-up.

The basset hound got slipped into Hannah's locker the next morning. She never acknowledged getting it back, but I hadn't expected her to.

The banana sticker was stuck on a postcard and mailed to Dylan. Let him wonder.

A few other items were left in lockers or mailed. When Christmas came around and we went to my aunt and uncle's house, some items were returned to my cousins' rooms. Only one was a true reunion—a plastic horse returned to a stable of other plastic horses that still took up a shelf in my college-age cousin Marguerite's bedroom. Other cousins' collections had disappeared.

K and I didn't talk much about collections after that. If they had doubts, I encouraged them to talk to me about them. And I shared my doubts too. Neither one of us was collecting them. Sharing is very different from collecting, and I was learning that I liked sharing much more.

I forgot all about the box of doubts. Time passed. Then, with a sensation that felt like suddenness even though it had been in front of us all along, it was time for us to head off to college. Different colleges, in different parts of the country. We were going to try to stay together, but didn't feel any certainty about it.

I went over to K's to help them pack. This prolonged the process considerably, because so much of our history was now a part of that room. Certain shirts and sweaters had to go to school with K purely because we associated them with specific nights, specific times together.

When I went to help clear out the closet, I found the doubt box sitting at the bottom, not unlike where the puzzle box sat in mine. The lock was in place.

"Oh!" I cried out. "You still have it."

K poked their head around the closet door to see what I was talking about.

"Oh yeah. Just leave it there."

I could have picked it up. Shaken it to see if there was anything inside. Checked the lock to see if I could get in.

But I left it alone. I bowed my head to it. I said goodbye to all such things.

Ring of Fire
by Jenny Torres Sanchez

The Matchbook

The unintentional collection started the night Lucia's mother died.

The small matchbook was on the floor, in the hallway just outside of the hospital room from where nine-year-old Lucia had just been rushed out by a nurse.

"Wait here, my dear," the nurse said. She'd been calling them that for weeks—Lucia's mother, father, and Lucia herself. *My dear.* Lucia loved and hated it. It was nice. But also Lucia didn't feel dear to anyone, especially not a stranger.

She watched as the nurse rushed back into her mother's room. Lucia could hear the commotion clearly, and she wished she'd made herself small enough to go unnoticed, shrunk into the corner of that room so she could stay close to Mamá. She hurried to the small window looking into the room before another nurse in the hallway noticed and quickly ushered her away.

"Don't watch, my dear," this nurse said gently before turning into another patient's room. Lucia sank down onto the floor in the hallway and waited.

That's when she saw the matchbook—black and crisp, with words that read DIAMOND CLUB—in the opposite corner. Lucia stared at the shimmering silver letters as machines beeped louder and voices rose and spoke more urgently from the other side of the door. Something called a rapid response team was called over the intercom. Then a Code Blue. More medical staff appeared, sneakers squeaking, running down the hallway and into her mother's room.

Lucia focused on the matchbook. She thought of the sound each letter made. Saw them in her mind as they had been on the walls of her first-grade classroom. She conjured up the glossy posters of a D—*dog*, an I—*iguana*, an A—*apple* . . .

There were beeps and buzzes and rings and intercom static and then . . . then there was deep silence. Lucia knew what it meant but could not look away from those matches. She felt the weighty stare of each nurse and doctor as they filed out of her mother's room. One of them knelt down next to her, patted her arm. *I'm sorry, my dear,* he said.

When they were all gone, Lucia reached for the matchbook and shoved it into the small pocket of her jeans. Only then could she look toward the room. Slowly, she made her way to the door, peered through the window, and saw her father standing over her mother's body. She waited. For him to turn to her, to gesture for her to enter, to make room there for her too, next to her mother's bed to say her final goodbye.

Finally, he turned and walked toward Lucia. Then out of the room and down the hall toward the elevators without so much as a backward glance. Lucia knew she was expected to follow. So she did.

A week later, Lucia's bedroom caught fire.

The Candle

"Is your birthday not coming up soon, Lucia?" Ms. Janie peeked over the fence that divided their yards one summer day before Lucia's eleventh birthday. Their neighbor was older and had been friendly with her mother, but Lucia had never spoken much to her. This year, though, Ms. Janie was intensely interested in gardening and was always out in the yard.

"How are you celebrating?" Ms. Janie asked, clipping a weeping bougainvillea that was hanging slightly over the fence into their yard. Lucia shrugged as she watched the papery flowers fall.

She didn't tell Ms. Janie how she'd missed her tenth birthday because it was just a few weeks after her mother's death. Lucia didn't know if her father had forgotten, or if it was his way of punishing her for the fire. Either way, she was somehow sure her birthday would go unmarked again this year. And she was glad.

Lucia had never had many friends, but after her mother died, the few she'd had didn't know how to treat her anymore. They faded into the background of life. She would see them at school, of course, and sometimes they even spoke to her, but mostly they were ghosts who just floated around here and there. Besides, she couldn't imagine anyone coming to her house. It was small and dark and her father's presence filled every space. God, no, she could not imagine any of them inside there singing "Happy Birthday" to her and eating cake.

Though she wondered if maybe Leo and Cleo would show up again. Her imaginary friends from years ago had shown up the night of her tenth birthday. They were still small, six, the age they'd been when they had visited Lucia every day. The night of her tenth birthday as she lay in bed, they opened the door to her closet and came out, set up their old table for tea parties, and brought the biggest sprinkled cake she could imagine. She'd been touched they still remembered her years after she'd forgotten them. But she could tell they were a little uneasy around her now, so much older, different. And after the cake and nervous smiles, they'd slipped back into her closet and never come out again.

"Wait here, I'll be right back," Ms. Janie said. A moment later, Ms. Janie was lowering a small gift bag over the fence to her. The bag was a bit crumpled, and Lucia could tell it was reused, maybe the gift inside too, but she didn't care. It was still pretty, and the heftiness of it sent a shiver of anticipation through her.

"Go ahead, open it," Ms. Janie said. Lucia reached into the bag and retrieved a candle. She lifted it to her nose and took a whiff. It smelled sweet, like cookies.

"Thank you," she told Ms. Janie. She did not tell her she was not allowed to have candles since the fire. Or that she loved the way it smelled. Or that it made her miss her mom. Or that it made her want to ask Ms. Janie if maybe she could live with her until she turned eighteen.

"Of course," Ms. Janie said, and went back to clipping her plants.

Lucia put the candle back into the bag and thought about lighting it later that night, secretly, while her father slept.

The Lighter

It was a gift from Felix. Or at least, it was something he provided.

He worked at Vinnie's Vinyl—the record store Lucia would sneak off to when she couldn't stand her father's heavy presence anymore.

Felix was two years older and had gone to her school the previous year, but was now, as he put it, *out in the real world.*

She got a small thrill every time she walked into the store and saw his messy hair somewhere in the aisles or behind the counter. They chatted more each time. And then, one day, they were making out in the backroom, intoxicated by the musky smell of incense and only vaguely aware of the buzzing sound that cut through the music in the store when a customer entered.

During that time with Felix, Lucia had felt free. And oh, how she hated that the feeling came from making out with a guy. She had promised herself she would never be the kind of person who needed a guy. She'd seen her mother need a guy, sacrifice herself for Lucia's father, and she was not going to do the same. But Lucia also didn't want to give up this feeling. She spent several nights trying to figure it out, wondering if she should go to the store the next day for that rush she felt, before finally deciding she didn't feel free because of Felix—she felt free because of herself. She felt free because she was doing what *she* wanted.

She wanted to make out with a guy in a back room.

She wanted to let him touch her in all those places that electrified her.

She wanted to get lost in the beautiful euphoria of physical attraction.

She wanted him.

And when she felt the lighter in his shirt pocket one day—retrieved it and marveled at its simple beauty—she decided she wanted that too. She ran her finger over the glossy red-pink-and-green exterior and stared at the burning sacred heart in its center.

"For me?" she said.

He laughed. "Sure, keep it. To remember me."

The words struck her as odd, and only later did she think it was maybe because he had already met the college girl he eventually told Lucia about. She appreciated that he'd wanted to *let her down gently*, as he put it, and she acted as if she didn't care. But it stung. Not because she loved him, Lucia decided. But because of the sudden loss of closeness, of being something to someone.

Maybe I did love him, Lucia thought sometimes when she lay in her bed replaying their kisses and the feel of him, the way he looked at her. She couldn't be sure. Love was something Lucia only vaguely remembered feeling.

At any rate, she avoided Felix and the record store after that. She never wanted to seem like she was looking for a pity make-out session. Or give Felix the notion that she needed him. Instead, Lucia decided she didn't need anyone.

And she swore never to set foot in Vinnie's Vinyl again.

Johnny Cash

Mamá loved him.

When Lucia's father went to work, Mamá watched from the living room window as the car drove away. Then she'd slowly walk over to the record player, slide the record out from the stack, and carefully place it on the turntable. Lucia loved the sacred silence as Mamá carefully set down the needle, the slight crackle just before the opening of the first song. And then his voice.

How it filled the house. And made Lucia's mother's eyes light up.

She'd look over at Lucia and wink playfully. So Lucia came to love him too—Johnny Cash. She even wondered if maybe Mamá had once known Johnny Cash in real life. When she stared at him on the album cover, she would think of her mother in his arms. When she heard his songs, she imagined he was singing them to her mother. And she wondered if maybe Johnny Cash was her *real* dad. Lucia thought of this as they danced and laughed as loud as they wanted. It didn't even bother her that sometimes Mamá's eyes filled with tears as she sang about shooting a man just to watch him die or walking a line, because even as her mother cried, she seemed happy and . . . *alive*. It was the only time there was light and sound in that house. It was the only time Lucia remembered breathing easy.

She hadn't heard that voice since before her mother got sick. But there it was this morning—playing in her head, startling her awake. She couldn't place it at first. All day, the same frustrating section skipped on loop in her head until finally, as she washed and dried a dish she'd just used for lunch, the first line came to mind and slipped from her mouth: "I keep a close watch on this heart of mine . . ."

So immediate, so vivid and bright, was the memory of her mother that the dish fell from Lucia's hand and crashed to the kitchen floor as she ran into the living room, certain she would find Mamá there with the younger version of herself. Instead, Lucia stared into empty space. For a moment, several moments, she stood perfectly still, feeling.

Mamá? she whispered.

She didn't know what she expected. She hadn't let herself think about Mamá much over the years. When she did, her father's presence became more unbearable, and she felt abandoned, and the prohibited, unthinkable anger her father had forbidden her to express grew inside her.

But today, Lucia remembered. And she wondered where they were—the record player, Johnny Cash, and her mother.

She began to search the house, and hours later, she found the record player and records, shoved into a black garbage bag in the corner of their crowded garage. She hauled the player upstairs to her room and then went back to sift through the records, finally finding Johnny in the rubble. Like most of them, the vinyl was bent and warped and unplayable.

Lucia felt a hot flash of anger.

She should go clean up the dish she broke. She should go and put everything back in its place from when she tore through the house looking for Mamá's things. She should start making dinner. She should.

But she didn't.

The Record

She opened the door to Vinnie's Vinyl, and the familiar buzzing sound sent a small wave of shame through Lucia. Especially when she saw Tony, not Felix, at the register. Tony, who had caught the two of them in the back room and then always made the same joke when he saw Lucia.

"Well, well, well . . . Loosey Lucia," he said as she entered. He laughed. She ignored Tony and headed straight to the records. Flipping through Brandi Carlile and the Cars, she finally found him.

It wasn't the same album Mamá had played all those years ago. It was a compilation. *The Essential Johnny Cash.*

Lucia ran her finger over the word "essential," turned the album around to scan the song titles on the back, and felt an intense sense of power and remembering. Especially when her eyes fell on one song in particular.

"Hey, I got something I gotta grab in the back room . . ." Tony said, rushing past the narrow aisle, brushing his hand against her thighs. Lucia turned, imagined pushing him to the floor. Imagined him jumping to his feet, staggering backward, his face red with embarrassment as he retreated. But instead, she watched him disappear into the back room, his laugh trailing behind him.

Lucia's face burned. Why didn't she *say something, kick the ever-living shit out of him*? She hated the way she never acted on or said the things that came to her mind. The way she always pushed them down, ate her words and policed her own actions.

She turned back to the album in her hand, studied the price tag. There was no way she could afford it. But Johnny Cash stared back at her, and she thought of how her mother listened to his music in secret.

Go on . . . The words were so clear, Lucia looked around to see who had whispered them. But she was alone.

Go on, Lucia . . . She didn't know if it was Johnny Cash talking to her, or her mother, or that voice in herself she never listened to. But she did know she had to have this album. No matter what. She deserved this fucking album. So before she lost her nerve, Lucia clutched it to her chest and walked out the door.

Lucia rushed home and began to hurry upstairs, but the thought of the mess she'd left in the garage, in her father's bedroom while looking for the record player, stopped her. She had to clean it up.

And then she was hungry, so she made herself a grilled cheese sandwich. And then her father was home, so she made one for him too, as was expected. And as they sat in awkward silence, it seemed to her that they had arrived here at the kitchen table together as if by accident and destiny.

Lucia stole looks at her father and thought of her mother. She could not understand how Mamá had fallen in love with him. She could not remember him treating her with much kindness or consideration. Everything always was about him.

She wanted to tell her father then suddenly about how her mother listened to that old Johnny Cash record with only her. How they'd had fun even though he couldn't stand it. How, just now, she remembered her mother even put on a bright red lipstick for Johnny Cash. And she'd never seen her mother happier than those moments.

Lucia thought of that being the happiest her mother was allowed. Of all the hours, all the times, her father crushed potential happiness out of her mother and Lucia in this house. How he was the only one who had a say in anything, ever, the only one, even, who got to say goodbye to her.

The image of him through the hospital window sparked into Lucia's mind. And then, she remembered the fire.

"Dad . . ." she started carefully. "Tell me about the time my room caught fire."

Shortly after the fire, Lucia had asked him to tell her the story. She was fascinated this had ever happened to her but genuinely couldn't remember it. And anytime she asked her father about it, he met her questions with anger, so she hadn't broached the subject in years.

He was quiet for a long while. Lucia waited.

"That never happened," her father answered finally.

Lucia met her father's gaze; he stared at her defiantly. It'd been a long time since she'd looked him in the eye. And when she did, something in her burned.

Lucia picked up their plates, washed them, and went upstairs to her room.

The Fire

It'd been years since she'd thought of it. She had a *sense* of that day but could never hold on to the details. There was something about it she wanted to understand. But now her father refused to even admit it had happened.

Maybe it made him feel like a bad father. And Lucia wanted to shout that he had been. Maybe it made him feel like a bad husband. And Lucia wanted to shout that he had been. But after all her father had been and all he had not been, he owed her this at least, didn't he? She deserved her fire story. Not his absence, not the look he gave her when he was present—lips pinched as if he were physically trying to contain . . . *What was it? Resentment? Hate? Jealousy? Disappointment?* She'd caved in and cleaned up the mess she'd made searching for the record player, hadn't she? And for years, *years*, she'd quieted her thoughts and questions. For years she'd washed dishes and cleaned and lived in service to her father and *his* anger, which snuffed out the oxygen in this house. She'd been a good girl, damn it, just like her mother had always asked her to be. Just how her father demanded she be.

Lucia picked up the record from her bed. She unwrapped and

removed it from its sleeve and breathed in the distinct smell of melted plastic. She'd hidden the record player in her closet, and now she leaned down before it, placed the record on the turntable, and checked that the volume was turned down as low as possible. Just before setting the needle down, she closed her eyes for a moment in anticipation of the sacred silence before the music, and that's when her mother's bright red smile flashed briefly in her mind.

The vision was gone quickly, too quickly. But Lucia remembered the lipstick she bought when she dressed like a flapper for Halloween last year and hurried to the top junk drawer of her dresser. There she found the small tube of lipstick and a compact mirror. Carefully, Lucia applied the bright red just as she remembered her mother doing, and she studied her image. She smiled. Playfully winked at herself. And then, there she was, her mother.

Lucia felt something inside her ignite.

She put away her lipstick and mirror and, as she did, noticed the matchbook she hadn't paid attention to in years. Next to it, the lighter Felix had given her. And there in the corner, the candle Ms. Janie had gifted her. Lucia stared at the three items, which, until that moment, hadn't seemed to amount to much.

But tonight, her eyes took them all in as one. Lucia reached into the drawer for the matchbook and, at its touch, heard the beeps and buzzes of the hospital. With them came a rush of more memories. She remembered suddenly so clearly how she'd come home the day of her mother's funeral, how she'd expected and hoped to see Mamá that day to deliver her delayed goodbye, but how Mamá had not been there, not the way Lucia remembered. And in her ear, she heard again her father's harsh whispered explanation as he sat next to her in the pew. *Your mamá was cremated. Burned.*

Lucia's body ached with the memory of wanting, of wanting to find and be with her mother, of wanting to *burn*. And how she had crawled under her bed in her little black dress and struck match after match, looking for Mamá in each flame, in the smoke, in the phosphorescent glow, until suddenly, one of flames touched the edge of her bedspread.

Lucia crawled out from under her bed and watched as the flames grew higher, as her room became aglow in fire and light. She searched, certain her mother was somewhere in that fire, waiting for her. And then her father came in and extinguished the beautiful flames.

Lucia opened the matchbook and stared. There, still, was a single match.

She reached for the candle she'd been too scared to burn years ago, too scared her father would smell the sweetness of it. She touched the match to the wick and delighted in the flare of it. Not wanting to blow out the match, she let it burn until it reached her fingers, and when it did, she thought of her mother. She tried to remember her voice, her touch, her smell. But all she could think of was how much she'd wanted to say goodbye while Mamá was still somewhere in that hospital room, in the air, before her essence dissipated and disappeared into some unreachable forever.

Lucia reached into the drawer and took out the lighter Felix gave her with the burning sacred heart image in its center. In the flickering glow of the candle, it seemed to gently pump with life. She thought of those paintings that if you stare long enough, you see something else in them and wondered if that was what was happening as she watched the heart pump harder, as the image of her mother appeared around it. And with the image, finally, the memory of *her*. Her touch, her smell, her singing voice.

Lucia hurried over to the record player and turned the volume knob all the way up. A small movement caught her eye, and when she turned, she noticed the ghost of her nine-year-old self staring back at her. Lucia took in her younger self, that girl without a mother, with an angry father, with no power or understanding of why things were the way they were.

She beckoned her, but the little girl wouldn't come. Lucia winked playfully at her, just as she remembered her mother doing, and then her small face broke into a smile and she walked over to Lucia. Lucia reached for her hand. Carefully, they both set the needle down on the last track of side B, and together they waited.

The blaring horns filled the room gloriously! Fire blazed in her younger self's eyes, and Lucia felt her own flash bright. Johnny Cash's voice filled her room, and the shadows created from the candle danced on her walls. Lucia watched as *the flames went higher* and felt the burn she'd been carrying within herself for years get hotter.

She took deep, sweet breaths into her body. Then more and more as she thought of fire and oxygen and heat and fuel. With each breath, she fed those years of her anger. She let it flash and flicker and flare. She felt it blaze and roar and, oh God, how good it felt to fuel this anger. To let it *live*. To let it fill her. To let her heart and body burn with love and rage and memory.

The heat raced through her arms and legs, crawled under her scalp and burst through, into wild flames around her face.

Lucia watched as her room glowed brighter and brighter, as her mother's voice and her voice and her young self's voice filled that room, all of them singing along with Johnny Cash. Louder and louder the horns blared. Brighter the room glowed. Hotter Lucia burned.

She reached out and saw flames bursting from her fingertips now, watched as tiny fires dripped to the floor and danced around her. She laughed in the delight and power she felt. In the astonishing happiness that it brought.

And then there *he* was, her father, at her bedroom door, watching.

The song finished, leaving only the crackle of needle on blank vinyl and fire. Lucia took in her father, the way he cowered by the door. He looked small and sad.

"I'm not afraid of you," she said. Then repeated it, again and again, gathering strength and confidence in each chorus. In her voice she heard theirs too—her mother and her younger self.

Lucia watched as he retreated from her, from her burning room. She reveled in the fear in his eyes and the trembling of his body. Then she watched as, one by one, the flames slowly extinguished themselves, revealing no burns, no scorching or damage.

And for the first time in a long time, Lucia felt love.

[Content warning: violence,
guns, hate culture, bigots,
assault, patriarchy, #metoo,
homophobia, transphobia,
hate crime, abuse, genocide,
fatphobia, mankind,
assassinations,
the unsinkable American dream,
and more of the same]

free admission
all hours
waking or not

welcome

there is no line outside
The Museum of Misery

only a picket of stanchions
one wears words like a hat

you head in

key

1. Atrium & Help Desk
2. Gallery A:
   Hall of Cultural Inheritances
3. Hands-On Exhibit
4. Body Shame Café
5. Gallery B:
   Hall of Personal Cost & Gift Shop
   Gender Is Your Role Theater
6. Children's Area
7. Human Rights
8. Emergency Exit

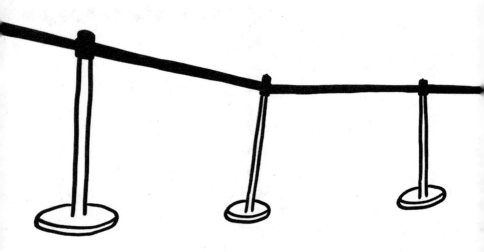

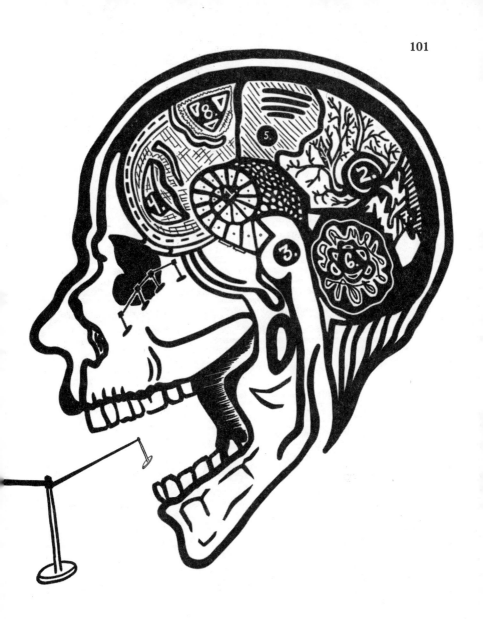

Atrium

Above the dome, the sky
Below the dome, the skeleton
That came out of their closet

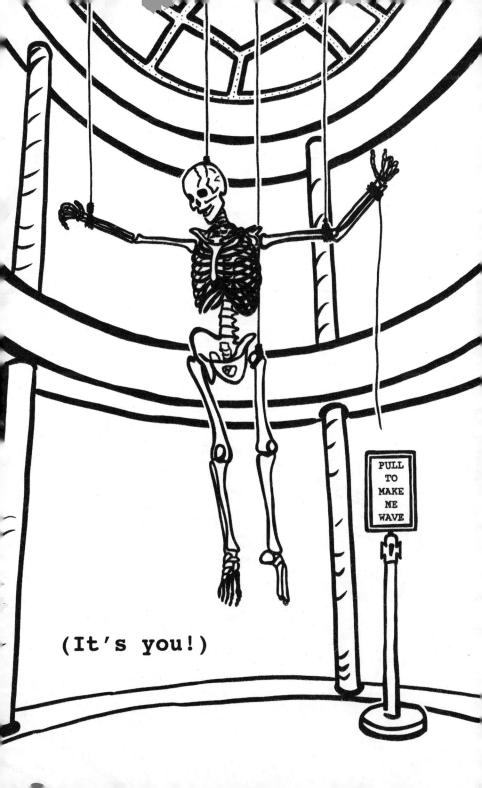

PULL
TO
MAKE
ME
WAVE

(It's you!)

Help Desk

The docent is your mother
"Back again so soon?"

She marks your card
Her brain can't see you

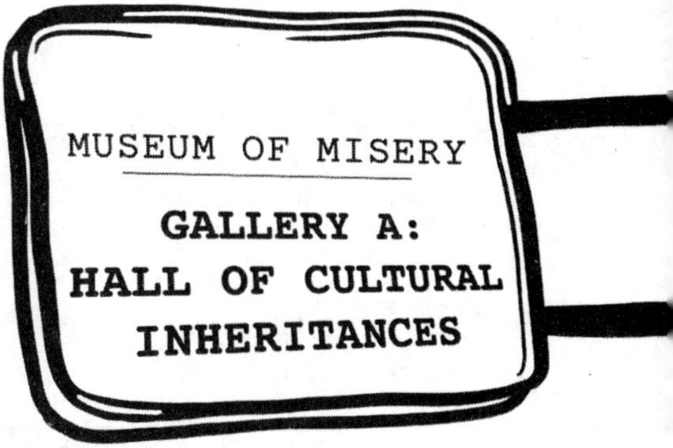

MUSEUM OF MISERY

**GALLERY A:
HALL OF CULTURAL
INHERITANCES**

"Under Pressure" on repeat

Remember AIDS?

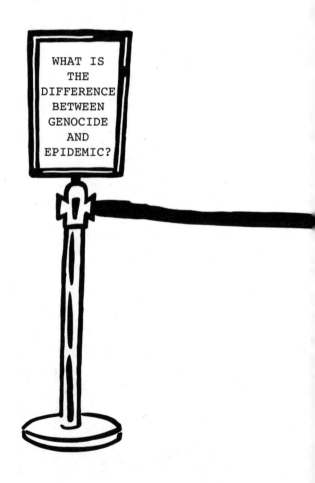

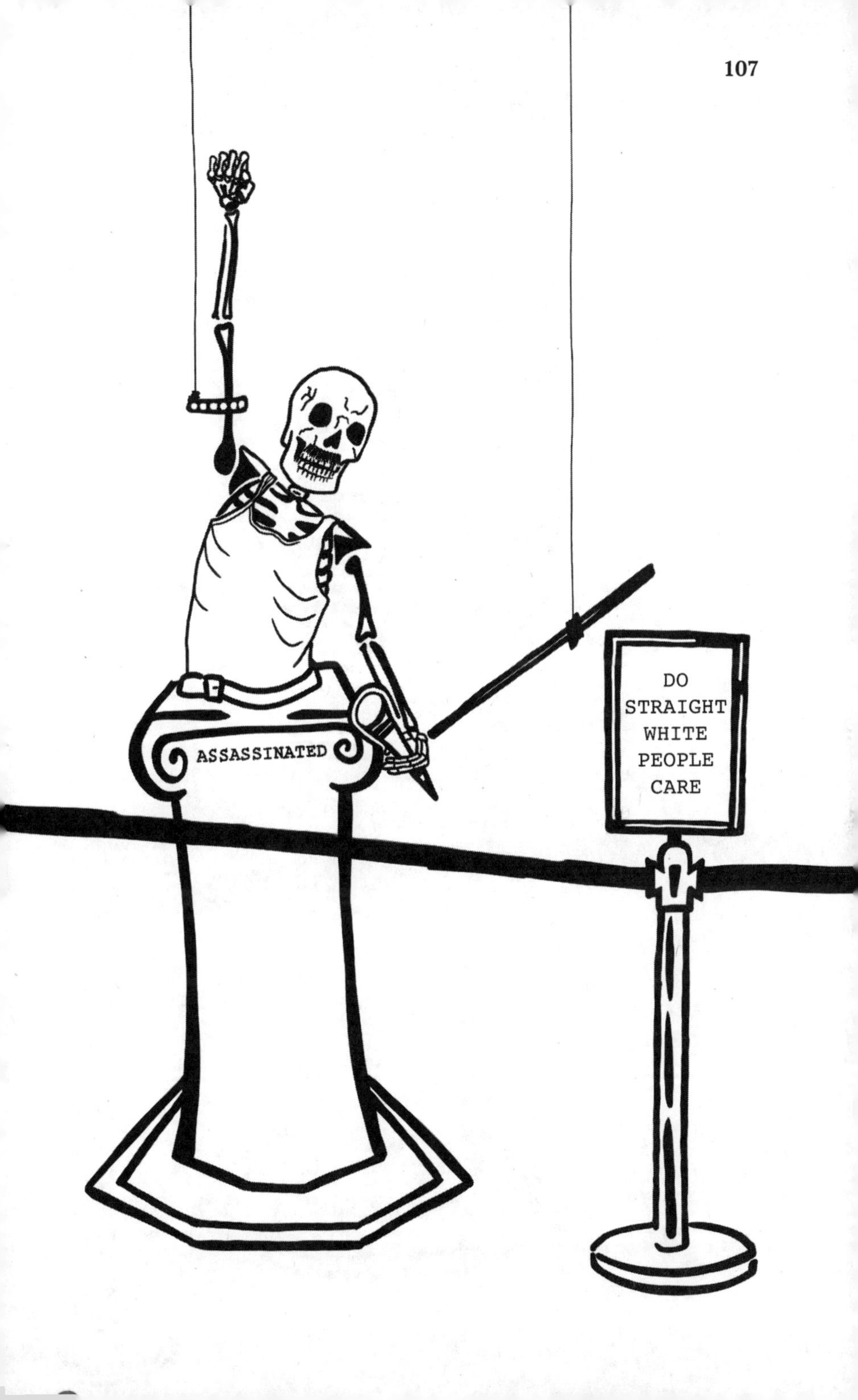
ASSASSINATED
DO
STRAIGHT
WHITE
PEOPLE
CARE

John Lennon didn't die
in iconic oval specs
They looked like this

(The price of being ahead of your time
Is a bullet to the mind)

Behold!

That requisite *Titanic* piece
In every museum
National metaphor of America
Post-iceberg, pre-tragedy
Full steam ahead toward bisection

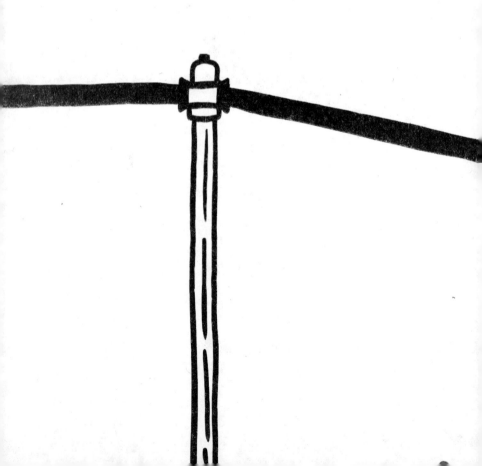

TITANIC
1972-CURRENT

WOMEN AND
CHILDREN
FIRST ➡

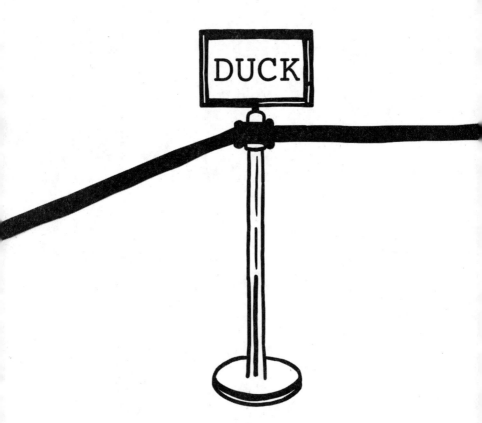

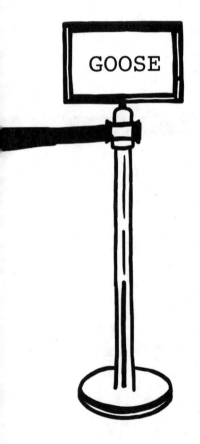

MUSEUM OF MISERY

**HANDS-ON
EXHIBIT**

hey.

you hungry?

MUSEUM OF MISERY

Body Shame Café

MEN
Meat, potatoes, chips, drinks, treats,
pizza. All you can eat.

WOMEN
Salad, wrap, grilled chicken six ways,
white wine OR one cookie. Price by pound.

KIDS
Blandness, Ketchup, Raised-in-a-Bubblegum Float.
Eat free, start young.

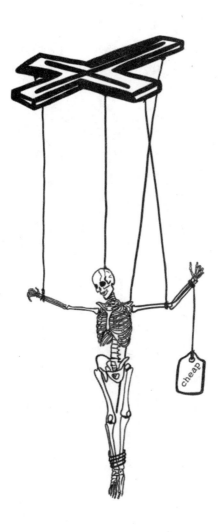

Concussion

Never forget the day you learned
Boys are allowed to hurt people

Don't you like what you're suppo
what you're supposed to? Don'
Don't you like what you're supp
supposed to? Don't you like wha
what supposed to? Don't
you're supposed to
you like what you'r
sed to? Don't you
you're supposed to
you like what you'
sed toDon't you lik
u're supposed to? D
Don't you like what you're supp
? Don't you like wha
e supposed to? Don'
Don't you like what you're su
supposed to? Don't you like wha
what you're supposed to? Don'
Don't you like what you're supp
supposed to? Don't you like wha

MUSEUM OF MISERY

GALLERY B:
HALL OF
PERSONAL COST

GENDER IS YOUR
ROLE THEATER

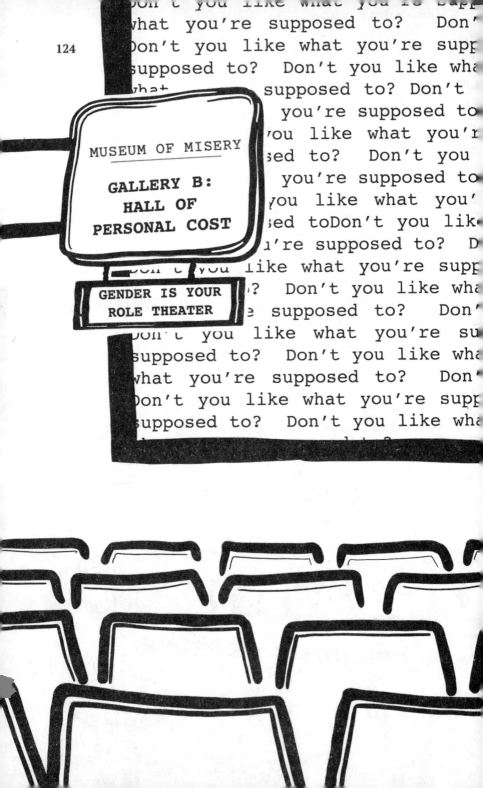

like what you're supposed to
to? Don't you like what you'r
're supposed to? Don't you lik
ike what you're supposed toDon'
't you like what you're suppose
posed to? Don't you like wha
what you're supposed to? Don'
't you like what you're suppose
pposed to? Don't you like wha
 you're supposed to? Don't yo
ou like what you're supposed to
to? Don't you like what you'r
're supposed to? Don't you lik
 like what you're supposed to
d toDon't you like what you'r
're supposed to? Don't you lik
 like what you're supposed to
to? Don't you like what you'r
're supposed to? Don't you lik

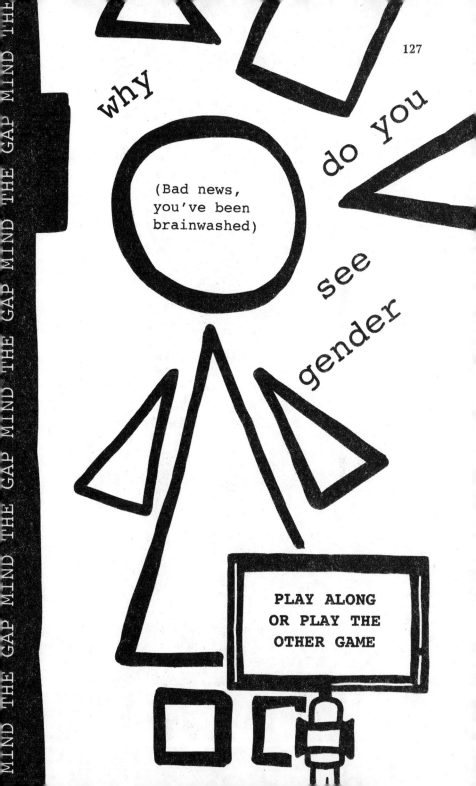

why do you see gender

(Bad news, you've been brainwashed)

PLAY ALONG OR PLAY THE OTHER GAME

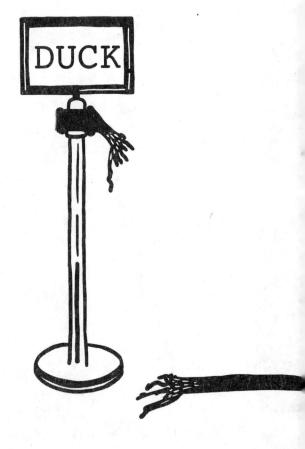

(It's you!)

hey.

you need to breathe.

IN TWO,

OUT TWO, TH

IN TWO, THREE, FOUR

OUT TWO, THREE,
FOREVER

THREE, FOUR

EE, FOREVER

IN TWO, THREE, FOUR

OUT TWO, THREE,
FOREVER

Did you know you can
abuse yourself?

Change your perspective.
Save your life.

Keep going.

Now make a new choice.
Turn this page.

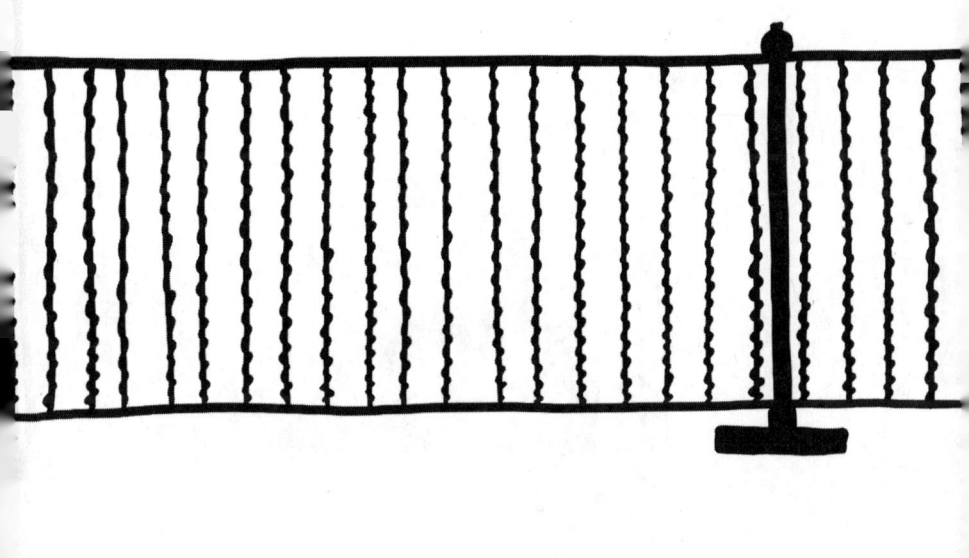

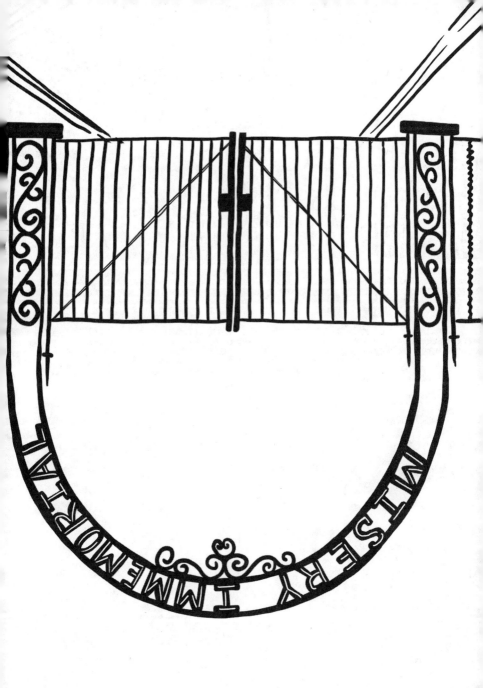

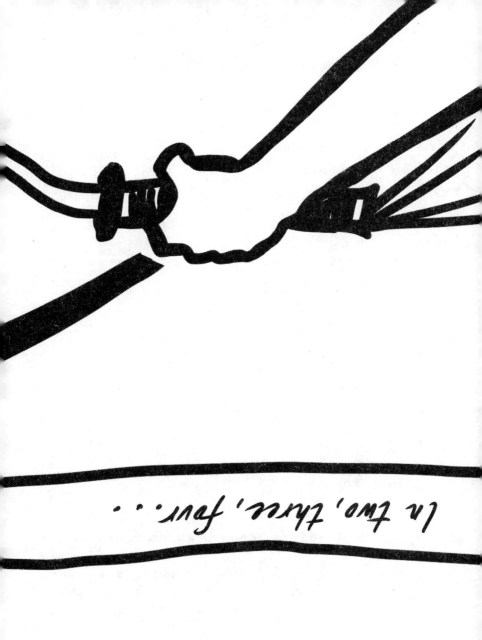

Un two, three, four . . .

This story is about reframing,
a key part to my survival.

If you're interested in renovating your own
museum of misery, I highly suggest the help
of a licensed mental health counselor.

You are the curator of your own mind.

-cory

p.s. There is no such thing as trans rights.
They're called human rights, and everyone
gets them. Or you are a bigot.

La Concha
by e.E. Charlton-Trujillo

This Is the Story of the Day Before I Leave

Today I'm building a tank. Tomorrow I'm leaving this town in it. Leaving and never looking back because that's what leaving is. Ask my father, whose wounds were so deep he had to find a surgeon who wasn't a surgeon to stitch him back together. Once he was whole, he never looked back. I can't wait that long.

Pues, I need a tanque.

This Is the Story of My Jar-Filled Closet

I've been collecting parts of myself inside the idea of my mother since she died. I started collecting them in a chipped-lip jar from a ditch near Gunner's Gas 'N' Go. I have a jar of glitter, a jar of beach sand, a jar of dirt from the Grand Canyon. Jars of mini-cars, mismatched buttons, broken beer bottle glass, stick-on stars, pencil shavings, unused Tampax. Jars of black and blue crayons, sewing needles, delicate thread. Jars of torn-out pages from books my mother read. A jar with a single strand of my hair, of postcards from people somewhere, a jar inside a jar full of fortune cookie messages. A jar of tears, a jar of laughs, and a jar of coins collected by my sister before she left. The more jars I stack in my closet, the deeper it grows. Now it's the depth of a football field. It's the only safe place in the house that is not my home.

It would've been a dream closet for my dead mother, who always wanted more space but settled for less. She'd stack barbells on top of fragile ornaments. Gourmet cookbooks on top of her abuela's hand-written recipes. Cardboard boxes of family photos buckled beneath bags of wadded-up new clothes. One day she shoved my father and me somewhere so far back that she forgot where we were.

I can't be like her.

I have to protect the things I love.

This Is the Story of Mi Hermana

She surprised me the day before she went missing with a greasy-bottomed bag from our favorite panadería. Two orejas pastries for me and a big-ass chocolate concha for her. She smiled all wild and alive. Scrolling through pics of Colorado, Michigan, and Maine on her cracked-screen cell phone. Saying she couldn't wait to get out of South Texas. To go somewhere like Muskegon, where there was snow and lakes you drive on. *Imagine a world where the walls don't always have ears and hands.*

She always talked in metaphor. Like life was one big, fantastic stanza. But something was different that day. I only know this because she didn't come back. It's easier to notice something then. When it's gone.

This Is the Story of My Dead Mother

If she were alive it would be a different story, but she's not. She's been dead since—

"Mía!"

"Not now!" I say to my dead mother.

She's dead. Not like traditional dead. Six feet deep in an overpriced coffin or cremated and collected inside a beveled jar or a used Bustelo can. That would make more sense, though. That kind of dead. She's just not here. She's not there either. She's in between, and that's how she's been since she invited Him into our lives without our permission.

This can be good for us, she said. *We'll never have to settle.*

This Is the Story of The Model Citizen

We moved into this house that is not our house but His when they got married. Then it was three-minute showers and three squares of toilet paper. His neighbors think He's the saint of Lectern Street. He has won the award for Best Front Yard three years straight. Earning Him a cash prize of seventy-five dollars each time. He keeps the money in a Christmas tin in His office, where He collects pictures of things He shouldn't. Where He makes bullets out of other people's mistakes and fires them in the court of public opinion. Where He measures the time it takes anyone to shower or shit in His house.

Today He's receiving an award from people who regard Him as a model citizen. People who don't live on this street. My sense is they are like a lot of people. They actually do judge a book by its cover, and His cover says all the things that make them feel like He deserves an award for something He's not.

This Is the Story of My Grave-Digging Brother

He's not my real brother, and sometimes I think he's not really a grave-digger. But he comes in late at night with dirt-trimmed nails, stained T-shirts, and muddy boots that used to be his dad's. Only his dad's feet were too big, so my brother wears them when he buries other people's love and his problems.

His dad—my stepdad—resented my brother the minute he picked up a shovel instead of a football scholarship. Even my dead mother had something to say about it from the beyond. As if he could somehow dig her dead self up. Some things just stay buried. Six feet below at the cemetery or in the sandbox in the backyard. Some kids make sand-castles in sandboxes. The neighbor's cat shits in ours.

This Is the Story of La Concha

I find a queen conch caked in caliche near the highway on my way to school. Cracked along the lip, but the inside? Flawless. Smooth. A shiny ombré of blush to pale.

I hold the opening against my ear the way they do in movies. Eyes close. Listen.

Hollow echo. A faint whistle, then . . . the roar of the Gulf. The reverb of laughter. Squeaking swing chains. Mariachi gritos. The breaking of—

I pull it away.

The swell of cars going somewhere not here returns. I trace my fingers along the rough ridges of the outer shell. Where has it been? What stories does it know? Is everything different on the ocean floor? It's the one thing I can't fit in a jar. I have to keep it close.

This Is the Story of The Pen Thief

"She's not my mother, because my mother is dead," I say to the school counselor.

I try to explain this as she looks at her smartwatch then back at me. People like my school counselor who steal pens from the equipment closet and use them to document the ways she thinks I'm broken never seem to care about the ways other people are fractured. Fractured and unset. Left to fuse back together crooked. Like my stepfather, who makes me call him "Dad," even though I already have one. Even if he never looks back.

I ask her, "Where did you get that pen?"

And she says, "Home."

And I know that's not true because I've seen her lift entire boxes when she thinks no one is looking, and I think about that as she tells me to be honest with her.

This Is the Story of My Poem Para Mi Clase

I stand in front of my English class thinking in Spanish. Thinking about my closet of jars and how I have to keep them safe. How the conch in my messenger bag will never fit in a jar. It's harder to protect things that aren't contained.

Mrs. Joyless waits for me to start reading my poem juxtaposing the institution of family and marriage. The word APATHY flickers on in the eyes of the kids watching me, only I don't know what it means because it was on a quiz I never studied for. And this is a poem I never tried to write because the institution of family and marriage isn't something I can write about. Mrs. Joyless doesn't care what we know, but what she can make us believe.

I look at the blank paper in my hand, and just before I sit down and take the zero, I think about the striations of amber, rust, and tangerine wrapping the outside of the conch shell. And I escape inside the smooth opening, slide along the canal, and the sound of my sister's voice and her stanzas call out.

"Es Un Día Como Cualquier Otro."

Mrs. Joyless interrupts, "In Eng-lish, Mía."

It's a Day Like Any Other Day

The Magician takes the stage.
Rabbit
Hat
Everyone claps.
Pleased.
It's a day like any other day.
Sawing her in half.
Everyone claps.
Pleased.

Even as she gasps.

It's a day like any other day.

He makes them all disappear.

Everyone claps.

Pleased.

Even though they aren't . . .

Here.

There is no any other day

when the Magician has His stage.

Fuck around and find out.

He'll show you

What to believe

This Is the Story of Being Sent Back to The Pen Thief

She asks me if I'm getting enough sleep. Am I drinking enough water? Do I "consume caffeine? Tobacco? Alcohol? Are you sexually active?"

"You can't ask me this. None of it."

She mangles my name in her mouth like she's chewing rusty thumbtacks. She pretends she's a doctor, ready to diagnose me with her stolen pen and sloppy cursive. Because that's how doctors write, all messy, but she's not a doctor. She's not even a surgeon not surgeon, and that's exactly why I don't trust her. She wears her heart in her head behind a vault—gunmetal-gray steel and concrete. She doesn't let anyone inside. Maybe not even herself. Maybe she's dead like my mother. If not, she's on her way.

This Is the Story of Elote Man

The Elote Man isn't like the others in town. He doesn't lie. He doesn't steal. He only collects coins, cash, and the currency of story. I would elect him presidente del mundo if there were such a thing because he's creative, joyful, and everything my sister loved before she didn't come home. Plus, he has a really sweet goatee.

Elote Man calls out to me, "¿Qué pasa, Reina del Cuento?"

He always smells like tamarindo and tamales. Like butter and buñuelos. Like the idea of something you can't own or invade.

"What can I get you?" he says.

"Elote cup. Extra heat."

"That's the Sin and the Saint," he says, smiling. "Lust in a cup. Dusted with rust."

Elote Man likes to speak in poetry—in rhymes. He pretends he's on a stage. Big bright lights. Microphone. Sometimes una guitarra. A trombone. A marimba. Una tamborita calentana. He spits out words between cutting lemons and squeezing limes:

> You gotta be a Mexican
> with something bigger
> on your mind.
> Commerce is one thing
> but greed divides.
> ¿Qué hora es?
> *No sé.*
> Simón . . . ¡Órale!
> Life's yours to define . . .

He's refined. Smooth. Seventh grade last time in regular school, but smarter than most dudes. Words learned from thrift store dictionaries and library downloads. He stands proud, scooping corn into a cup. Not afraid to wear his heart on his sleeve, but smart enough to keep his eyes tattooed to his back. Wish I could be brave . . . like that.

"I almost forgot," he says. "Para tu colección."

He holds a scuffed peso between his nub of a thumb and bandaged index finger.

"1944," he says. "Cool, right?"

"This is valuable. You should keep it."

"Pues, I done told you. Those blanquitos go on vacation. Cozumel— México City. Always come back and try to drop 'em on me like they're nickels. Remember that guy I tell you about? With the shoes."

He hands me my cup. "Shiny Feet?"

"He gave me a 1921 Silver 2 Peso today." He laughs all big and full. "Simón, that shit is value. Guy at the pawnshop gave me four hundred and fifty. I know it was worth more, but he gotta make money too, ¿qué no?"

"True."

"Pues. Haven't heard nothing about your sister."

I stay quiet for too long. People don't like quiet. It makes them want to fill space where there should just be space. Only he doesn't. He waits.

"No one has," I finally say. "Maybe she's run off to Michigan. Colorado. She said people were always happy in a place where it snows."

"I don't know," he says. "Está frío. Even in the summer sometimes. But right now? December?"

I stare down at my corn cup.

"You know," Elote Man says. "No shame in being scared. In being worried about her."

"I'm not scared."

That's a lie. I lied a lot more since my sister hadn't come home. Since my mom lost her life, and my stepdad's feet got too big, and my brother couldn't stop digging toward the center of the earth. Thinking if he could get there, he could feel something hotter than his own anger.

"I'm almost done building my tank," I say.

"Remember, mijita. Un tanque is a weapon. Even without a gun."

This Is the Story of The Model Citizen and Me

My stepfather sits at the dining table airing out his feet. His socks draped over my chair. His shoes in my seat. I pretend not to see them. I pretend I'm with my sister in Colorado at a Christmas carnival eating sugar cookies and drinking hot cocoa. Talking about how much we hate the way people look at us here—in His town—but not in Colorado or Michigan or Maine because no one can be sad there. No one can say your back is wet and your shoes are small. Even the snow feels warm because we belong.

"Where have you been?" He asks from the bottom of his feet.

"school."

"It's 5:11."

"studying."

"Where?"

"school."

"Why are you lying?"

I close the curtains in my mind. Pretend I can't feel His voice vault across the kitchen table, scale the length of my back. The timbre of each word hooks into my spine. Severing the vertebrae at C5. The paralysis is quick. I whisper to myself, *This is not real.* I can't cry for help. Crying is for white girls in old horror movies. Not for Chicanas like me with a stepfather like Him.

This is where I go quiet. Pretend I'm making snow angels in a field blanketed in white. The way my sister talked about snow. That it's a warm dream that doesn't melt. We shape two snowwomen side by side because women together can multiply. Hold the line.

I smell the moment of Him and forget the moment with Him. Count to one thousand and eleven when I finally realize I am alone.

This Is the Story of Building a Tank

I have been building a tank since my sister went missing. A tank minus the gun turret. I have no use for a weapon like that. I don't want to kill; I just want to get out safe. Not like my dead mother. She had a gun that she kept in her closet before she married my actual dad. Before I began as a mistake in her belly. Then she had me, and I was her weapon against him. To make him marry her. To keep him obedient. To demand he give her the moon when he couldn't even afford the sky. She used me often, and with precision, so he had to leave to find a surgeon who wasn't a surgeon.

My sister said The Model Citizen liked that my dead mother was a wannabe sniper, but not the real thing. It's easier to control something that doesn't know its actual power. He stockpiled her ammunition with his White last name and bleaching of her past. She did a victory lap when we moved in. She doesn't know how many tunnels He has dug beneath the floor and between the walls. That each of them leads to every room my sister and I have slept in. Because how could a mother know such a thing and throw confetti when He walks in the door after work?

I had to build a tanque because she became smaller in this house big enough to brag about in a magazine, even with her tiny closet.

Smaller and smaller. Until one day, she died.

This Is the Story of My Grave-Digging Brother's Question

I'm midway in making a sandwich when my brother plants his muddy shovel against the granite kitchen island. Spear dripping dirt onto the porcelain tiled floor. He walks past me like I'm air. Jams a Klean Kanteen against the smart fridge water dispenser.

"You going?" I say. "To the award party thing?"

"Gotta work."

He gulps his water because he gulps everything. Cans of Big Red, Red Bull, Red Dog—his dad's red-faced expectations. He swallows the world in chugs—big guzzle, guzzle, guzzle. He's midgulp when he notices me staring and stops. "What is that?"

I follow his stare to the conch sticking out of my messenger bag.

"A concha," I say.

"Isn't that a pastry?"

"It's also 'shell' in Spanish."

He tilts his head, stepping closer. I slide the concha onto the island. He leans down, studying it. It's the longest he's stayed in the same room with me when he didn't have to.

"You know, a queen conch can live in their shell for like . . . thirty years. Even longer."

He chuckles. "Can't imagine living in this house for the rest of the year. Definitely not thirty."

He smells like dirt and sweat and tired people, and he just showered. And just as quickly as he was interested, he isn't. He scrapes the point of the shovel against the floor, leaving a trail of dirt as he clomps toward the back door.

"Backhoes," I say.

"What?"

"I thought they used backhoes. To dig graves."

"I like your shell. Concha. Don't let Him see it. He fucks up everything that's beautiful."

My brother has been digging his grave since before we moved in. Only the hole is never deep enough. Never wide enough. It's hard to fit an entire life of disappointment and anger into a single space in the ground.

Maybe he should build a tank. Build a tank and get out.

This Is the Story of a Party I Hate

I strategically place myself in the farthest corner from everyone fawning over The Model Citizen. They're hypnotized by Him. Laughing when He laughs. Swaying with His sway. Their eyes clouded in the spin of everything He's made them believe. Everything—

"Cranberry-fig goat cheese crostini?" says The Hors D'oeuvre Server with the crooked black tie.

"Uh . . . okay."

"They're actually kind of good," she says. "My mom caters. Is . . . catering. This— She needed help. I don't actually know what I'm doing."

"Me neither."

Synchronized quiet.

"My mother is the dead woman," I say to the server. "Standing behind the man with the award."

"How long has she been gone?"

"Few years. Since she got married to Him. Maybe a little before. I don't know. I *really* don't know anymore."

"Happened to my aunt. It's like one minute they're there and then—"

"Right?" I say.

"Was it hard? Losing her."

"At first," I say. "Now it's just normal."

"She looks good for a dead person."

"They always do."

"I'm sorry for your loss."

"Thanks. You too."

Unsynchronized quiet.

"I better go," she says.

"Do you want to see my tank?"

This Is the Story of The Hors D'oeuvre Server

I open the door to my closet. It's now the size of two football fields. There are bleachers on both sides for Home and Visitors. My jars of snow globes, kindling, my first baby tooth, a seedling—of everything and nothing—fill the stands, circle the track, and flank around me. An exhale of a breeze whispers my sister's best stanzas.

I invite The Hors D'oeuvre Server inside. She steps onto the lush spring-green Bermuda grass. Kneels down, listens.

"There's a story in the ground," she says.

I twist the lid off the jar of my sister's coin collection. Drop in the peso from Elote Man.

She follows me to the end of the second field where my tank—

"This is amazing," she says. "How did you build this?"

"It took a long time."

"It's so . . ."

"Right," I say, climbing inside. "I made it big enough for me and my sister. In case she came back before I had to leave."

"It looks bigger," she says. "You could fit a lot in here."

"Well, I'm taking my jars."

"I think you could fit more. It's really something."

"I didn't add the gun."

"You don't need a gun. You have a tanque."

She smiles, and I grin like it's ordinary. Like having an hors d'oeuvre server in my closet is every day for me. Only my sister has ever come in here. She's the only one who could understand.

I climb out of the hull. Hop back onto the field.

"Can I show you something else?" I say.

She nods.

I reach into my messenger bag and pull out the concha.

"Wow . . ." she says. "It's so . . . alive."

"I found it by the highway."

"You have to take this with you," she says. "Keep it close."

I get lost in the glints of sunlight shaped in her eyes.

in the deep end. I looked around, then I walked down the steps to survey the inside of the pool. Actually, it was more like a third full. That shouldn't be too hard to deal with.

I stood there at the base of the steps and imagined me with my board, dropping into that bowl and sailing up over the pool light in the wall like Tony and his friends. It looked kind of tight, not quite the kidney-shaped Dogbowl. I ran my hand along the side wall; it was so smooth. I'd never been vertical before, but the magazine made it look like it was possible. I saw the ball floating in the middle of the water. Instead of trying to get it, I left it there. I hated my sister and her kickball friends anyway.

"Well?" they all asked when I got back to my house.

I grinned like a fool. "The only problem is we have to get rid of the leftover water," I said.

I grabbed a bucket out of the garage, and this time, we just climbed over my fence. We stood on the lip of the pool, staring at the possibilities. We'd never bailed out a basement or a boat, let alone my neighbor's pool.

"Is this kind of like stealing?" asked Alex.

"Getting rid of rancid water sounds like a service to me," said Skeezer.

We all agreed borrowing someone's pool was not the same as stealing it, so we moved on with our plan.

"Isn't there a plug or something you pull, like in a bathtub?" asked Bobby.

We looked at the grubby water and decided we'd pick short straws to find out. We had no straws, so we found some dandelions, blew off the puffballs for good luck, and used the stems. Skeezer got the short end, and he glared at us like we had stolen his lunch money.

This Is the Story of Elote Man's Question

I'm halfway back to the party I hate when Elote Man pedals his cart beside me.

"¿Qué pasa, Reina del Cuento?"

"No sé."

"It's late for you to be out."

"I have to go back to a party I hate."

He considers this, rubbing the length of his goatee. "A fiesta of misery. Doesn't seem like a fiesta."

"No. It isn't."

"How is your tanque?"

"Bigger than I thought," I say. "I showed it to a girl."

His grin multiplies uneven.

"I felt like she could see it."

"Could you?"

I think about his question because some questions are thinking questions. Even if they seem like they're not.

"I think so. Maybe."

"Mijita, un tanque es muy fuerte."

"But you haven't seen it."

"Verdad. Pero I've seen you. What else could you build?"

I laugh to myself.

"See you mañana," he says. "¿Está bien?"

"Mañana."

This Is the Story of the Party I Hate, Again

I am not the elephant in the room, yet everyone is staring at me, their wide eyes dilated like I make them see blurry.

My dead mother weaves through the partygoers toward me. They don't notice her because she's not with Him. She is a visibly invisible thing only me and The Hors D'oeuvre Server collecting empty plates across the room can see.

"Where have you been?" my dead mother asks, looking past me.

She knows I'm here because everyone else is staring at me.

"Your father has been looking for you." She waves to someone behind me who doesn't wave back. "He's gone home to get you."

"Mom . . . ?"

"He's gone home to get you." She smiles. "Go home and tell him you're sorry."

The floor springs open, and I drop. Free-fall. Through the blue sky, through the Bermuda grass, through the house that was a home with my actual father, through me sitting with my sister eating panadería pastries, through one of my jars—shattering the glass bottom—and land feetfirst on my bedroom floor.

The closet door is wide open. My stepfather, sheathed in darkness, stands inside. Back to me. Broken jars at his feet. Their lids scattered. Parts of myself everywhere. Hemorrhaging, and I don't have a surgeon not surgeon to stitch me back together.

This is the day I'm going to die.

He turns. Glass crackles under His big, shiny shoe.

"Where were you?"

"These are my things."

"Where? Were? You?"

He throws a jar against the wall behind me. A feather flutters out and onto the floor.

"This is my house." He steps closer. The floorboards wailing beneath his feet. "You don't have things. I give you things. I show you things. I own you."

I close my eyes. Pretend I can't smell His Jack Daniel's breath and sweat soaked in lies. That the walls don't have ears and hands—*This is not real.* I can't cry for help. Because no one would believe a girl like me who collects herself in jars in a closet while building a tank to roll over everything that has ever hurt her.

I can't get away from His hands—Him humming "The Star-Spangled Banner"—I try counting, but I forget all the numbers. I am screaming in my mind, crying.

I fumble for the concha in my messenger bag. I put it against my ear. Start to listen—

He snatches it from my hand. Shoves His fingers inside the opening. Holds it up like it's a joke. A fucking joke!

I rush at Him. I fight to take it back. He holds it just out of reach.

"It belongs to me," He says.

I have to keep it safe. I have to try and . . .

This is the beginning. This is the end.

This Is the Story of the Day Before I Leave, of My Jar-Filled Closet, of Mi Hermana, of My Dead Mother, of The Model Citizen, of My Grave-Digging Brother, of La Concha, of The Pen Thief, of My Poem Para Mi Clase, of Being Sent Back to The Pen Thief, of Elote Man, of The Model Citizen and Me, of Building a Tank, of My Grave-Digging Brother's

Question, of a Party I Hate, of The Hors D'oeuvre Server, of Elote Man's Question, of the Party I Hate, Again

This Is the Story of . . .

"No!" I scream, and that's when it happens. I scratch Him across the face, and before He can finish anything He imagines, there is a reverb.

The ringing metallic sound of my brother's grave-digging shovel connecting to his father's skull. The Model Citizen drops to the floor. A thick pound echoes from knees. He wobbles. Startled. Confused.

Then deflates.

My grave-digging brother stands over Him. His shovel slips from his hands, clangs to the floor.

My hands shake. I look at my brother.

"Are you okay?" he asks.

"No."

"I dug here as fast as I could," he says.

My brother and I watch Him writhe. Mumble.

I pry la concha from his sweaty, perverted hand.

My brother and I step over Him and into the closet. We lock the door from the inside. I hold la concha between us. We lean in.

Quiet.

Then.

"Do you hear it?" I ask.

"Snow."

Pool Bandits
by G. Neri

1976 was the driest year in the history of the world. It hadn't rained in Southern California since forever, and now it was summer, and the governor declared a state of emergency. Los Angeles became a desert, for real. People were forced to stop watering their lawns. Golf courses dried up and died. And if you were lucky enough to have a pool, you had to slowly "let it go," because refilling it was now against the law. So, by July, pools in our beach town sat half-empty, evaporating slowly in the sunburnt backyards that littered the hillside.

This is how it started. Me and Alex and Bobby and Skeezer skating through the endless lonely blacktop roads that wound through the meandering low hills near where we lived. Cruising those streets felt like surfing—or at least what we imagined surfing felt like. Surfers were badass and liked to beat on people who couldn't surf (like us).

Bobby's brother, Rory, practically lived in the ocean. I never saw him with dry hair or shoes. But Rory and his friends always made us feel like shit 'cause all we did was skate on our stupid clay-wheeled boards that we made in woodshop. We spent hours skating on the sloped driveways in our alley, pretending we were surfing the North Shore of O'ahu or some shit. They thought we were a joke.

"Jesus, look at you frickin' losers," Rory would say. "A surfboard with wheels is like a runner in a wheelchair. It's just sad."

We rode the streets like poseurs until one day I was bombing down a hill and a car suddenly pulled out of a driveway right in front of me. In that half a second, I knew I had two choices: slam into the side of the car like Wile E. Coyote, or bail.

I took one step off my board and flipped head over heels like I'd just stepped onto a treadmill going full speed. I skidded on my back across the blacktop, ending up right next to the car's passenger door. When I looked up, some old lady was staring at me out the car window, her mouth gaping wide like she'd seen someone get murdered.

I felt bad for some reason; I didn't want to scare the shit out of her and have her die of a heart attack or something. So I just popped up like it was no big thing and limped off. I didn't know where my board was, but I kept walking like this had been my plan all along. It was only after I got home I noticed I was only wearing one shoe and the back of my shirt was practically destroyed—ripped open and replaced by black tar and dried bloody skid marks. That was the end of my street-bombing days.

· · · · · · · · · · · ·

When we heard about a cement drainage ditch up in the hills on the south side of the bay, we knew we had to skate it. Alex found out its secret location through some dirt biker kid who sold him pot, and we rode our bikes for almost two hours to get there. Then we had to hike through the scrub and tall weeds over some never-ending hills. It was hot, and I was ready to give up 'cause we forgot to bring anything to drink. But then Alex got to the top of the last hill and started jumping up and down like he'd found treasure.

Most people wouldn'ta thought twice about some stupid ditch. But to us, it was like we'd stumbled across Disneyland, if Disneyland had been a secret and we'd found out where it was. The cement ditch was about two hundred feet long, sloping down the canyon with banks on each side. Since there was no rain, the thing was bone-dry. Someone had even swept it clean of sand and dirt—at least on the upper half. We grabbed our boards and ran to the top of the ditch. Alex got first dibs 'cause it was his find. But even from where I stood, I could see the cement was rough and there was no smooth transition to the banks.

Alex started at the top, dropped in, and got in two good turns before he wiped out, hard. He grabbed his board and threw it out into the dirt, trying to act like he wasn't crying. Bobby went next and got in a third bank before he face-planted. My back was still stiff with scabs from my street fall, so I let Skeezer go. He didn't make it past the first turn—hit a small rock, which sent him flying. No more ditch hunting for me.

• • • • • • • • • • • •

Toward the end of the school year, we had built a little wood ramp in woodshop to skate on. We didn't finish it, but Mr. Holland had left it in the woodpile in back of the classroom, so we snuck it over the fence and took it home, where we finished it up with some of my dad's tools. We stuck it in my driveway, but my dad hated the noise of us riding up and down all day long. We moved it over to Bobby's house but decided it kinda sucked, so we talked about doing a small heist at a construction site for plywood and two-by-fours to build an even bigger, better ramp. But Alex was an altar boy and didn't want to go to hell for stealing, so we backed off.

It was shortly after that day that two things happened around the same time that changed our lives forever. First, we heard about these new skate wheels made of polyurethane that were extra wide and used precision bearings to give you an insanely smooth ride with extra gripping power. They could even go over bumps and rough terrain.

We ran down to the surf shop, which was the only place that carried them. Unfortunately, Rory and his buds were there talking to Ben, the board shaper, who was blasting Zeppelin's "Kashmir" on an eight-track player. When we walked in, they stared us down like we'd invaded their private club. As the music swirled and spun out of control, I thought they'd kill us right there. But Alex didn't care. Even from the door, we could see those gleaming red wheels behind the glass case. He practically drooled when he leaned over the glass to stare at the future.

The second thing was those half-empty pools that littered backyards around town. One day, I was in the liquor store and saw an issue of *SkateBoarder* on the magazine rack. On the cover was a picture of a long-haired skate rat named Tony Alva. He seemed to be levitating 'cause he was riding vertical in what looked like an empty pool. I opened the magazine and ripped through the pages until I came across the headline: "Dogtown Boyz Hit New Heights." The image showed Tony and his crew of Z-Boyz standing at the bottom of an empty pool while another skater named Jay rode over their heads barefoot, blue-tiling it on the pool wall.

My head exploded. What the hell—*vertical*? I'd never seen anything like that. They were just street punks like us, maybe a little tougher and rougher, but still, *vertical*?

I knew I had to show my friends, so I swiped the magazine and some Pop Rocks and raced over to Alex's house. It was the first week of summer, and he was chilling in his room listening to Boston's "More Than a Feeling" over and over. When I showed him the article, I could see his brain starting to spin. At first, he seemed confused, but then I saw the light bulb go on.

We gotta find the others.

I called Skeezer and Bobby, and we all met at my house. Before that, only Alex had the new wheels on his board, but when Skeezer showed up, he had them too. Only they were mounted on a Zephyr fiberglass-molded board, which made my homemade plywood board look like 1972.

We pored over the magazine. Apparently, a friend of the Dogtown Boyz had a pool. When he found out he was sick with cancer or something, he talked his dad into letting him drain the pool so him and his friends could skate there. He called it his Death Wish.

The Dogbowl became Dogtown's official hangout, and we knew we had to find our own Dogbowl if we were ever gonna be cool like them.

Then it hit me. My neighbors had a pool, and I knew for a fact they were on vacation over at Lake Powell. They'd be gone for a good two weeks. I barely knew them (their kids were Preps), but if we were gonna be badass like the Dogtown Boyz, we needed our own pool to skate in. Then even Rory would respect us. (Better yet, I could see Tony and Jay befriending us and beating up Rory just for dissing us.)

After hearing my brilliant idea, the guys elected me to scout out the scene next door. If I got caught, it'd make sense 'cause I lived next door. Maybe we could kick a ball over the fence and then I'd just be retrieving it? We tossed my sister's red kickball over for my alibi.

I knocked on my neighbor's door and waited. No one answered. The house was dark. So I walked around to the side gate and let myself in like I was just the kid next door fetching my lost kickball. My heart was racing. But when I made it to the backyard, it skipped a beat.

The pool was oval, like a pill. It wasn't deep, maybe six feet on the far end. It looked half-full of murky water. I walked to the edge and glanced down. The steps were bone-dry, with my sister's ball floating in the deep end. I looked around, then I walked down the steps to survey the inside of the pool. Actually, it was more like a third full. That shouldn't be too hard to deal with.

I stood there at the base of the steps and imagined me with my board, dropping into that bowl and sailing up over the pool light in the wall like Tony and his friends. It looked kind of tight, not quite the kidney-shaped Dogbowl. I ran my hand along the side wall; it was so smooth. I'd never been vertical before, but the magazine made it look like it was possible. I saw the ball floating in the middle of the water. Instead of trying to get it, I left it there. I hated my sister and her kickball friends anyway.

"Well?" they all asked when I got back to my house.

I grinned like a fool. "The only problem is we have to get rid of the leftover water," I said.

I grabbed a bucket out of the garage, and this time, we just climbed over my fence. We stood on the lip of the pool, staring at the possibilities. We'd never bailed out a basement or a boat, let alone my neighbor's pool.

"Is this a kind of like stealing?" asked Alex.

"Getting rid of rancid water sounds like a service to me," said Skeezer.

We all agreed borrowing someone's pool was not the same as stealing it, so we moved on with our plan.

"Isn't there a plug or something you pull, like in a bathtub?" asked Bobby.

We looked at the grubby water and decided we'd pick short straws to find out. We had no straws, so we found some dandelions, blew off the puffballs for good luck, and used the stems. Skeezer got the short end, and he glared at us like we had stolen his lunch money.

Finally, he kicked off his slaps and walked slowly down into the water. It was pretty rancid, so he acted all worried, like there might be sea monsters or something down there. When he got to the drain, the water was up to his waist. He looked unhappy, feeling around with his toes.

We looked at each other. "You gotta go down and pull out the plug, you dope."

Now he really hated us. "Fuckers."

"Hey, short straw, bitch. Them's the rules," said Alex.

We started snickering as Skeezer lowered himself into the gunky water. "Stick your head in so you can see what you're doing," I suggested.

He took a breath and went under. When he came up, he was pissed. Turns out, there is no plug at the bottom of a pool.

We laughed our asses off. He refused to talk to us for about an hour.

We searched around for a switch or something that would drain it but didn't find anything. Finally, we decided to try the bucket. We devised a system: one person would scoop water, hand it to the next guy, and he'd hand it to the next until someone up top grabbed it and poured the water into the bushes.

At first it was kinda fun. We tried singing like the chain gangs in the movies. But after an hour of this, the pool still looked the same. Finally, Bobby said this way sucked and that he had a better idea. He looked around and pointed to a rolled-up hose on the wall.

During the gas crisis two years ago, his brother, Rory, made him siphon gas out of someone's tank. He almost upchucked when the gas poured into his mouth. But it worked, and he figured the same thing would work for pool water. He stuck one end into the yellow water and stood with the other end by the fence next to the alley. He sucked and sucked on his end, all while Alex made blow job jokes to us on the sly.

After about ten minutes of sucking, Bobby spit up water and it came pouring out of his nose and mouth. It was funny as hell except we were so stoked that it worked. Water kept flowing out, so he threw the hose over the fence and let it drain into the alley. But then I said it might attract too much attention, so we fed it into my yard instead. Later, we went back to my house to chow down on Cap'n Crunch and SpaghettiOs. We played Ping-Pong, read through my collection of *MAD* magazines, and just waited it out.

Four hours later, Alex did a spot check and told us to grab some towels and a mop. I grabbed my mom's mop and some bath towels out of the pantry. He made us mop and soak up those towels until they were filthy. My mom would kill me for ruining them (and flooding her rosebushes with chlorine), but it'd be worth it.

By the time we were finished, it was dark already. We were jonesing to skate it, but even we knew riding in the dark was a stupid idea. We decided we'd rest up and meet back in the morning.

That night I couldn't sleep. Around two in the morning I got up, grabbed my blanket and pillow, and snuck over to my neighbor's yard. It was a bit weird. What if I ran into someone actually trying to rob the place? But it was dead quiet. I made a little bed at the bottom of the pool and stared up at the moon until I fell asleep.

. . . .

"Get up, Gio, it's time for school," someone whispered sweetly into my ear.

I opened my eyes only to see three butts staring back at me.

Fuck! Skeezer farted in my face before I could get up. But I accidentally kicked him in the balls, so I got him back.

"Very funny," I said, rubbing my eyes.

I refocused and saw where I was, and everything came flooding back. We stood there as the sun started to creep up over the fence. It was like magic. Our own pool!

We looked at each other, and I knew everyone thought the same thing: How do you skate like the Dogtown Boyz? How do you get vert?

I grabbed the magazine, and we studied the pictures like it was a how-to manual for flying. I knew the first one to get vert would be the leader of the crew. I grabbed my board, but instead of starting from the top, I walked down to where the drain was and plopped my board down. I stood on it, feeling the cement, imagining myself doing the action. Alex interrupted my zen state.

"Um, dumb shit, you ain't getting vert like that," Alex said.

I ignored his ass. Then I slowly pushed my way toward the wall in front of me. My board went up a few inches, and as I was coming down backward, I rose up the back wall behind me and shot forward again. But I leaned too far back when I hit the wall, and my board shot up in front me. I tumbled, hitting my scabs. Then I spotted the board flying back down the pool wall toward my head—

Alex intercepted my board with his. "You're not getting anywhere with those wheels. Try my board. From up there," he said, pointing to the others.

He helped me up and shoved his board into my chest.

"Act like Tony," he said.

I went about halfway up the pool and turned. I imagined how Tony looked and felt on his first try. I put the board down and kicked off with one push. I could feel those wheels gripping. It was a smooth ride. I headed to the right and then pretended I was dropping into a wave. I slowly went in a half circle and suddenly I was heading back up toward them.

"Did I get vert?"

They laughed. "No, you rode around the drain," said Bobby. "But it's a start."

We all took turns, studying the grade of the wall. It wasn't the best shape for skating, but it was ours. We took baby steps, and nobody got killed (or vert). By lunch, we all were riding about three feet up the wall. By dinner, we were up to four feet, just below where it went vertical. We all took falls, but we were heading into unknown territory, so the scrapes and bruises became badges of honor.

We skated all day. At sunset, we voted and decided to call it the Butt Bowl, not only 'cause of this morning but 'cause we felt like we'd gotten our butts kicked and now we were kicking it back. By the end of the week, we'd be blue-tiling it and riding the lip of the coping along the top, taking pictures with Alex's camera and submitting them to *SkateBoarder* to show Dogtown how we did it down in the South Bay.

We also vowed not to tell anyone. If word got out, not only would we risk getting busted, but I'm pretty sure my parents would kill me. When my brother got caught for growing weed on our roof, he was grounded for four months with surprise room inspections.

The next day, we skated from sunup to sundown. Anytime we got too rowdy, I had to remind them to keep it down. Someone's gonna hear and narc us out.

That narc turned out to be my sister, Lisa, who'd been spying on us from her tree house—the one *I* helped her build. Traitor. She was gonna rat me out unless I gave in to her demands: One, she'd get to choose what TV shows we watched for a whole week. And two, she had a friend, Jenny, who skated, so we'd have to let her try the pool too.

I took a few deep breaths so I wouldn't go ballistic on her. TV—okay. I'd force myself to watch the *Brady Bunch Variety Hour* so she could get off on Greg (barf) singing. But to let another skater into the Butt Bowl—and a *girl*, no less (especially one of her friends)—*no*.

We had a code, and that code was sacred.

But that night at dinner, she started asking my mom about the neighbors, and as soon as she mentioned the pool, I caved.

The next morning, she and two of her friends showed up. She was playing that Elton John song "Island Girl" on her little tape player. She was pushing it.

I had to explain to my guys what the deal was. They couldn't believe what was happening. We were bound for greatness, and now we had to teach this *girl*? We looked back up at Jenny holding tightly on to her plastic penny skateboard.

"Don't worry," I said, "she won't last two minutes before she falls and goes crying back to Mommy."

I took it upon myself to set the rules. I told Lisa to turn off the music and explained the number one rule: *What happens in Butt Bowl stays in Butt Bowl.*

She made a face at the name, but I made my own back. "You don't like it? You can leave now."

"It doesn't even look like a butt," she said.

I rolled my eyes. She wouldn't understand. We made them sit on the deck chairs and watch. She was bopping to KC and the Sunshine Band just to see how far she could push me. Skeezer had just discovered the Ramones and started singing "Blitzkrieg Bop" even louder, and I told them both to knock it off. I reminded them we had to keep it low-key if we didn't want the cops showing up. I could see her friend Jenny was scared shitless. If only she was pretty and older than twelve, then maybe I wouldn't mind showing her the ropes.

Our goal was to get over the pool light in the deep end. Whoever did that first would have bragging rights over everyone else forever. We spent all morning trying to get there, but only Alex grazed the bottom of the light. For a few hours, we all ran straight into it and bailed from five feet up. It seemed impossible.

Then Jenny's sister, Cherie, showed up.

I'd only seen her once, at the mall, when we ditched the girls to sneak in to see *Jaws*. Other than her red hair, she hadn't struck me as anything special, but in the eight months that had passed, she had grown into a total babe, and we all stood there staring like idiots. She seemed annoyed by the attention, given she was seventeen and we were all fourteen. But suddenly skating didn't seem so important.

"Take a picture, why don't you?" my sister said under her breath. That broke the spell.

"Who else did you tell?" I glared back while trying to look cool.

That's when Cherie spoke. "Don't worry, I won't tell on you."

Then she sat down on a lounge chair, waiting. I imagined her sitting by the pool in her bikini.

My sister tried to egg Jenny on, saying, "If you're gonna try, you should try now." I could practically see Jenny's knees shaking. There was no way.

But then her older sister got up and asked, "Maybe I could try?"

I almost shit myself. I couldn't tell if she was joking or not, but she started walking toward me.

"Um, do you know how to skate?" I asked.

She laughed. "I don't know, do I?" she said.

I tried laughing it off and said, "We've been skating here two days, so if you're not willing to fall, I wouldn't—"

"You wouldn't, would you?" she said as if we were having a different conversation.

She came down the steps. The others cleared the way. I noticed she was wearing Vans and the toe of her right shoe was worn thin.

Cherie stopped in front of me. I could smell her sweat mixed in with the grape Bubble Yum she was chewing. "Is that your stick?" she asked.

I heard Bobby whisper, "Or is he just happy to see you?"

I nodded.

"Can I ride it?" she asked.

I almost lost it. I feebly rolled the board over to her and stood there like an idiot.

Cherie kick-flipped it up into her hands and checked out the wheels. She frowned.

Alex jumped in, offering his board instead. "Forget that. You probably need a man's stick."

She spun one of his wheels and smiled. "Smooth," she said. "But just 'cause you got a big board doesn't mean you got a ride for me."

Burn.

I laughed while Alex stewed, but Cherie still took the board and dropped it to the ground, catching it with her foot. She did know how to ride.

She jumped on and we laughed 'cause she was a goofy footer, facing the opposite side from what we all did. But then she started kicking around the flat of the pool, turning back and forth, even doing a slow, sexy 360. Alex and I looked at each other and shrugged.

Cherie skidded to a stop and faced the deep end. "Over the light?" she asked.

"Yeah . . ." I said, "but nobody's done it yet."

She studied the curves. "That's 'cause I haven't tried yet," she said.

She put her foot on the board like she was ready to drop in and—

"*FREEZE!*"

Cops! Three of them were poking their heads over the back fence from the alley.

We scattered like ants, taking off down both sides of the house. I thought about grabbing Cherie, but my stupid sister was standing there frozen, and I knew I had to save her first. I grabbed her and her friend and started shoving them toward our escape.

We ran down the side, and when we hit the driveway, I had to force her to take a left into our open garage. Her friend followed, but the others scattered, jumping on their boards and taking off down the hill. I grabbed the garage door and quickly pulled it shut.

Everyone went silent. We heard some footsteps and the police radio go by as the cops went looking for us.

"Over there! To the left!" I heard a car drive by, then—silence.

"What about Cherie?" asked Jenny, worried.

Hopefully, she got out with the others. Jenny wanted us to go look for her, but I made everybody stay inside and wait till the sun went down. My sister was staring daggers at me, but I just stared back.

"It was your idea to come. If you can't do the crime, don't do the time," I said.

"You got that backward, dickwad," she said.

We laid low for a couple days, but we'd all gotten a taste of the high, especially Alex, who was chased on his board by a cop car for about ten minutes before he cut across the park and lost them. It was rad, like being in a movie or something. We were so hooked.

But that pool was blown now. The neighbors would be notified, and we'd play innocent and not answer if the cops knocked on our door. We'd have to find a new pool. But this time, my sister would not be invited.

. . . .

We took to the streets ourselves, using our bikes to avoid standing out as skater suspects. Alex figured out just by cruising houses on the street, you could tell which places had pools: there was a white plastic drain hole that came out of the curb. We cruised around making a list of houses that had pools, and then we did recon to see what kind of pool they had.

I'd gone by a pool construction business and snagged a brochure. There were all kinds of pools: Lap, Roman, Grecian, L-shaped—all bad because they were unrideable shapes with ninety-degree walls with no bend. The rideable ones, rounded with drops into a deep bowl shape, had names like: Mountain Lake, Figure 8, Lagoon. But the real prize, the perfect pool to skate, was one called the Kidney. If we found a kidney that we could drain and skate, it would be a summer to remember.

Recon involved checking out backyards and making assessments (as any good detective knows). Sometimes, you could just peek over the back fence and make a judgment call. Maybe there were cement steps built into the pool wall, ruining the flow. Maybe the stagnant water was too nasty. Or there were cracks or flaws that made the ride impossible. We'd cross it off the list.

Other times, we did what came to be known as the Frisbee maneuver. We'd toss a frisbee over the wall of a backyard, hopefully into the pool, then knock on the door to ask if we could fetch it. If the mother was home, they usually didn't mind. We tried not to be too weird about it. But we were able to make a good list just on our side of town.

The other key we learned was to talk up the mom (or better yet, daughter) about upcoming vacations. Usually, if they let us into the house to get to the backyard, we'd notice something, a souvenir or something from a trip, and ask them about it and, if we were charming enough, talk about a vacation our family was going on so we could find out if they were going on vacation too.

This part of recon, I kind of liked. It was spy stuff, pretending to be something you weren't. Also, I kind of became interested in things I saw in their house and how different they were from my house.

We started a game. *Trophies*, Bobby called it. We had to steal one thing on the way through a house and not get caught. Something stupid, like a saltshaker or a trinket or a magazine. We had a little box of keepsakes we kept at my house.

But one time, I saw the mother doing laundry, and I gotta say, she was kind of hot, not like a mom—or at least not like *our* moms. And as we were passing through, chatting (Alex usually threw in something about church to make us sound trustworthy because he was an actual altar boy, at least inside church), I saw a bra hanging on the chair, and I don't know why, but I just grabbed it and stuffed it in my pocket when she wasn't looking.

I didn't think anyone saw me, but after we retrieved the Frisbee and determined the pool was a three (we'd devised a five-star rating system, one being pass, five being perfect), Alex pulled me aside and said, "You're gonna share that, right?"

I tried to act like I didn't know what he was talking about, but I could see he knew that I knew that he knew, so I nodded and said sure and that was that. But I slept with that bra that night and, um, things may have happened.

. . . .

Within a week, we'd made a master list of three- and four-star pools. A five would be an automatic next mission, but for some reason, fives weren't showing up in our neighborhood. We used the lingo we read about in the magazines: nasty water became worm juice, filtration holes became death boxes, the stairs were wedding cakes, the deep end, bowls. We started calling out tricks we hoped to do like off the lip, frontside kickturns or Bertlemanns, just 'cause the Z-Boyz did it.

Out of a list of thirteen rideable pools, we knew three of the families were going out of town soon. So we called the operator and asked for names and phone numbers by address. Me, having the most mature voice (since mine had dropped first), would call the numbers like I worked for the phone company, saying we had to work on the lines and asking if there were any dates they might be away in case the technicians had to come inside. This only worked twice, so those two pools got the next windows in our calendar.

The first pool was at the Woodson house over on Fourth Street: a Figure 8 pool with an eight-foot bowl. They'd be gone for a week to San Diego, so we did some recon on their street, playing Frisbee every afternoon while waiting for them to pack up the car and drive away. The Woodson pool was already about 80 percent dried up, so the job would be quick. They had a high fence and old neighbors who seemed to be hard of hearing. We watched the Woodsons drive off (Alex waved), and we grabbed the hose and went to work. Luckily, the houses were all single-story, so nobody would be looking down on us.

This time it took us two days to conquer the light. It was Alex, of course. But we were all so stoked I didn't get jealous. He walked us through the movement and was able to do it again. Skeezer did it next after four tries, and Bobby almost got it.

When it came my turn, I guess they caught me dreaming about Cherie. I was imagining her sitting on the lounge chair watching us, and I wanted to show her I could conquer the light too—hell, maybe even hit the coping with an off-the-lip frontside kickturn. So I grabbed my board, and next thing I knew, I was flying up the wall. It was like slow motion, sailing up the poolside and seeing the light pass under me as I flew around the bowl. I came back down and skidded out onto my butt, but it was good enough. We all high-fived and celebrated by going to my house to smoke some of my brother's weed. Next time Cherie showed up, I'd be ready.

· · · · · · · · · · · ·

The next day, we skated till we got hungry around noon. We were too lazy to go home or run over to 7-Eleven. We were determined to hit coping, but we needed fuel. Alex asked me to go into the house and see what they had to eat. He said it as a joke but not really a joke. But I didn't mind trying. We had drained their pool, right? What's a missing peanut butter sandwich gonna matter?

The first thing I did was look by the kitchen door and guess where I might hide an extra key. Under the mat would be too easy. But the flowerpot was looking a little out of place. First of all, the flowers were fake, and it just sat there in a place no one would stick fake flowers. Sure enough, I lifted it up and there it was: a key. I held it up for them to see, but they were too busy skating and egging on Skeezer to hit the tiles under the coping.

I looked around to see if the coast was clear. Then I let myself in and stood by the door making sure the Woodsons weren't going to walk in suddenly. It was super weird being in someone's house without them being there. The first thing you notice is their smell.

Every family has a different scent, and it kind of gives each house a special smell. The next thing you notice is all the stuff people use. The garden shoes by the back door. The recycling bin filled with Coors and Fresca cans. An ashtray with butts in it. They read *Motor Trend*, *Tennis*, and *People* magazines. In the *TV Guide*, someone had marked a page of an interview with Chico of *Chico and the Man* (with underlined text).

I went to the kitchen and opened the fridge. I was surprised how empty it was. No bologna or Cheez Whiz or anything good. They had a couple cans of tomato juice, a bottle of Tab, some celery sticks and cottage cheese. I scoured the pantry for some good cereal or something but all they had was Special K and *granola*. Finally, I scored a can of Pringles and a bag of marshmallows.

On the way back out, I casually checked the freezer hoping they'd have Fudgsicles or something. There was a tub of Neapolitan ice cream, but when I grabbed it, something rattled around inside the tub. When I opened the top, I found a plastic bag, and in that bag was a roll of dollar bills wrapped with a rubber band.

It caught me off guard. Who keeps money in the freezer?

I held the roll in my hand. The outside bill was a twenty. It seemed heavy, like a few hundred dollars maybe. Or more? A thousand?

I imagined what I would do with the money. Split it with the others? Buy a new board with those new wheels? Buy a used car? It kind of freaked me out after a minute. Who were these people? Maybe they were drug dealers or part of the mob or something. So I wrapped it back up and put it back in the carton and shoved it back in the freezer. I didn't tell the others. They'd be happy with the Pringles.

We skated all afternoon, getting higher and higher. Soon, we were touching the blue tile under the coping on most tries. When the sun started going down, we joked that we should just move in for a few days. Then we could just roll out of bed and skate. It'd be like a sleepover but with no parents. Then we just looked at each other and grinned.

"Fuck yeah! We should totally do it," said Alex. I guess he didn't consider that stealing either.

The money thing had me a little worried, but I didn't want to bring it up. We checked out the bedrooms and saw there were three. Skeezer wanted the master bed on account of we'd made him dunk his head into that nasty water. Fair enough.

There was one room that belonged to a boy. He had Dodgers posters and that smoking-hot Farrah Fawcett poster we all had. Alex snagged that room.

Bobby wanted the couch 'cause of the TV, so that left me with the daughter's room.

They made fun of me, saying I deserved it because of the incident with my sister, but it was in the daughter's room I discovered her stash. I mean, it looked like a teen girl's room, but then I started snooping around (not in a pervy way, just curious. It's not like I was gonna take anything).

I thought about my usual hiding spots. Under the mattress? Too easy. Top shelf of the closet? Nope. Her dresser caught my eye. I glanced through her drawers, but there was nothing interesting. When I got to the bottom drawer, I accidentally pulled it out too far and it plopped onto the ground. When I tried to put it back into its slot, that's when I noticed Amber's stash in the space underneath.

I knew her name was Amber because that's where she hid her diary too. The first page said: *If you are reading this, consider yourself dead.* That made me laugh. I imagined her finding out and hunting me down at school, but anyone named Amber was not gonna intimidate me. I wasn't interested in reading about her girl adventures, but the other stuff down there intrigued me. It was a little twisted, to be honest. A razor blade. A bottle of prescription diet pills (uppers, I figured) and a small bag of pot. But the purple vibrator? That was a little too personal.

We realized that we shouldn't turn on all the lights or we'd attract the neighbors. So we closed all the blinds and just turned on a small light here or there. We called our parents and told them we were having a sleepover at Alex's. Then we pooled our money and ordered a pizza. When the pizza guy arrived, we paid him and scarfed it down pronto. Then, because we were exhausted from skating all day, we crashed.

. . . .

In the middle of the night, I heard a sound that woke me up. *Voices.* But it wasn't Alex or Skeezer or Bobby.

Then I heard a man say, "Did you order a pizza before we left?"

Suddenly, I was wide awake with panic. *Fuck fuck fuck fuck fuck. They came back? Did they find Bobby?* He was asleep out there! I jumped up and opened the window as quiet as I could. There was a screen on it, and I tried to push it out without making too much noise. What about Skeezer and Alex? I thought about running out there to find them, but now I could hear the wife looking around, making comments.

"What? No, we didn't order pizza . . . Why is the room such a mess?"

Then I heard the boy: "Hey, somebody's been listening to my records—"

Shit, did the others ditch me and leave me behind to get caught? I looked around and all of Amber's stuff was still lying on the carpet. I grabbed the weed and forced the screen open. I was halfway out when the door opened.

I saw Amber's silhouette in the doorway. I froze, but it was dark, so I didn't know if she saw me. Then I saw she was about to scream—

"Don't," I said calmly, "or I'll tell your mom about your dildo."

She stood there in shock, and I was gone.

I was running. I left my shoes behind! *Shit.* Then I thought, *What about our boards?* They were all out by the pool. I thought about going back, but I knew that wouldn't end well. I ran home as quick as I could. I knew the cops would be scanning the streets for us soon. I stuck to the alleys and hoped the others would meet back at my house.

Out in my front yard, hiding in the shadows of our tree, Alex nabbed me and pulled me up into my sister's old tree house. Bobby and Skeezer were there too. So were our boards.

"What the fuck? You just left me?" I hissed.

Bobby had heard the car pull up and quickly woke up Skeezer, who then woke up Alex. Since my room was farthest away, they couldn't make it in time. They headed out the back door, grabbed the boards, and hoped I would make it out on my own.

I was pissed, until I remembered I did the same. I told them about my escape, the girl, and the dildo. Within a few minutes, we were smoking her pot just to calm down, but it was mostly seeds and stems. I knew we couldn't go home at three in the morning, so we just crashed in the tree house.

Skeezer was worried. "You know the cops'll be on the lookout now. Two emptied pools for skating? I bet we make the news."

"Maybe they'll give us a nickname . . . like the pool drainers? No, the pool thieves—"

"How about the pool collectors?" Bobby said.

At one point we heard a car coming down the street, and I peeked out. Sure enough, it was the cops. We put out the joint.

"Maybe we should lay low on the pools for a while?" said Skeezer, freaking out. "I don't wanna go to juvie," he whispered.

Bobby made fun of him, but I could see he was scared too.

Alex thought about it. "Naw, now we have a reputation to uphold. I mean, what fun is it if we let them shut us down?"

I laughed. "That's fucked up. We should play it cool for a while, then when it quiets down—"

"What would Tony Alva do?" Alex asked. "Let the cops scare him off?"

I thought of the Dogtown Boyz. Then I thought of Rory and his crew. *They'd all call us pussies,* I thought. "Fuck it," I said. "The cops won't catch us on our boards. Tomorrow, let's hit the Johnson house."

. . . .

The Johnson house was a last-minute addition that came across our radar because we had intel from the sister of the person house-sitting there. We didn't know the pool shape, but it felt like it had potential. The house was on a cul-de-sac that had a supermarket behind it. The house to the left was under construction (good for noise cover), and on the right was a park. Bobby knew the Johnsons a little through his dad, who complained how Mr. Johnson always got more vacation than him. He was jealous that they were vacationing in Hawaii too. But the kicker, the killer thing we found out almost by accident from Jenny, of all people, was that not only were the Johnsons on vacation, but Cherie would be house-sitting.

Which is how I ended up knocking on the Johnsons' door.

When Cherie opened it, she was still dressed in her pj's and had a bowl of Lucky Charms in her hands. She looked tired, like she'd been up late. It took her a second to recognize me.

"Oh, it's you."

She noticed Alex, Bobby, and Skeezer waiting at the end of the driveway. She took a bite of cereal, saw I was carrying my board, and did the math. I watched her chewing until she said, "You're not skating here," and started to close the door in my face.

"Wait," I said, sticking my foot in the door. "Just let me see it."

She looked at me like I was crazy. Then she laughed. "I saw you guys on the news this morning," she said.

I perked up. "Really?"

"Pool bandits . . . Jesus." She shook her head, then turned and walked away, leaving the door wide open for me.

Pool bandits? I thought. *Now that's like Jesse James shit.* I turned and gave the guys a thumbs-up, then followed her in. The place looked . . . lived-in. Her clothes and stuff were scattered around the floor. There was a Swanson's frozen dinner from last night on the coffee table in front of the TV.

"Bandits? Did they really call us that?"

"Something like that."

She stopped in front of the sliding glass door. I walked up beside her and looked out.

The pool was a kidney.

Holy fuck . . .

She glanced at me. "You can look, but no touching. I'm getting paid to be here, and I'm not about to let a bunch of freshman wannabees fuck up my jam."

I nodded and slid open the door, walking out onto the patio. It was a brilliant sunny day, the sky an impossible blue. Palm trees swayed gently in the breeze as I stepped up to the lip of the pool.

It was already empty.

I couldn't believe it. It was just waiting for us, perfectly primed like a gift from God. I dropped my board and walked down the pool steps.

"Don't even think about it," she said again, but it just blew past me like the breeze.

The pool was perfect in every way. Smooth, gentle curves, dropping down into a deep, wide bowl. I almost started crying. I walked down into the deep end, running my hand softly around its curves, imaging us sailing one after another over the pool light. The pitch was perfect. In this pool, we could even hit the coping—

"You know, you two should just get a room," she said.

I turned and she was standing at the edge of the pool. Her arms were crossed like she was going to enjoy denying me. But as we stared at each other, I saw a glint in her eyes that she understood.

"You could skate it too," I said. "You could be Bandit Queen."

I could see that hit her. She uncrossed her arms but had no comeback.

"How long are they going to be gone?" I asked.

She paused, unsure if she was willing to divulge. She slowly held out three fingers.

"Three days?" I said. She shook her head.

"Three *weeks*? Damn."

My mind raced as I slowly walked back toward her. She looked a little unnerved but determined. I thought about offering myself to be her personal servant or something, but she didn't seem the servant type. So I took a different tack.

"What if . . . we just skated . . . like, a couple days. A couple days, then we'll clean it up, scrub off every skid mark, making sure it's exactly as it is now?"

She didn't say anything. I could see her calculating the risk.

"And . . . *what if* . . . we came here once a week while you're here . . . and cleaned the house for you so it'll look perfect for when the Johnsons return?"

"Are you saying I'm a pig?"

"I'm saying . . . you probably have more important things to do than clean up after yourself." (But yeah, she was a pig.)

She wasn't sure if that was a compliment or not. Neither was I. She mulled it over a bit, but I could see her defenses weakening. Finally, I had one more thing to sweeten the deal.

"AND . . . I guess I could try to teach Jenny how to skate . . . ?"

She smiled, brushing the hair out of her eyes. "She's a wuss," she said, "but it's sweet of you to offer."

And with that, we had a deal.

. . . .

The Pool Bandits stood in a line around the shallow end of the pool. This was it: the place where we'd make our mark in this history of Southern California skating.

She'd asked us to come back in the afternoon, so I took advantage and splurged just for the occasion, buying a new set of polyurethane wheels for my board. They looked amazing, like they could handle anything. I didn't even want to ride them over. I wanted them fresh—virgin wheels for my big breakthrough. So I rode my bike.

"Who's going first?" asked Bobby.

I cleared my throat, knowing I was the clear choice—we wouldn't be here without me. But then Cherie stepped out with her board and announced: "Clear the way, pussies. Time to let the real deal in here."

We turned and she was decked out in her OP board shorts, Hang

Ten shirt, and checkered Vans shoes. Her hair was pulled back into a ponytail.

The guys all looked at me, like *Are we gonna allow this?* but I just shrugged: *Her poolz, her rulez.*

We stepped aside and she surveyed the pool herself.

I had to ask: "Were you gonna ride it without us?"

She smiled and shrugged. "You'll never know."

She walked down the steps, dropped her board, and rode down toward the bowl in one smooth motion.

She cleared the light easy. She immediately dropped in again—this time, backside!

My jaw must have been hanging down 'cause when she came back up, she put her hand under my chin and closed it.

"Why don't you show me what you got?" she said.

I don't know if she'd already been skating without us, but Alex and Skeezer egged me on, something about showing her what we're made of or some shit like that. I could still feel her hand on my chin and imagined for a second, if I hit a frontside kickturn off the lip, she'd look at me different, not as some fourteen-year-old kid, but as someone who wasn't afraid to push the limits. I didn't expect her to be my girlfriend or anything, but somehow I imagined she'd admire me enough to maybe give me a little action on the side?

I grinned at my own stupid thought and psyched myself up. Why not? I rode the tiles at the last pool. I was the brains of the outfit. The King Bandit. *Fuck yeah! I'll show you all what I got!*

When I think of the moment, it's kind of in slow motion. I push off on my new board, my virgin wheels sailing across the smooth surface of the pool. I imagine a giant wave rising up in front of me as my board shoots up, up, up into the vertical. I feel weightless as I go higher and higher—past the light, over the tiles, until I feel my wheels clip the pool's coping and then—its nothing but sky.

For a second, I am totally weightless—floating, actually. I look across and see them all looking up at me in awe—Skeezer cheering, Alex and Bobby high-fiving, and Cherie impressed. It seems like I am hanging up there forever, and I want to stay here, where everything is right with the world.

But then I shift my weight and begin to head down—without my board—and that's when everything goes silent and I float down down down into the darkness . . .

· · · · · · · · · · · ·

I'm asleep in bed. At least I think I am. Then I hear voices. Feel someone tugging at my hair. I open an eye, and I see Cherie kissing me, deep and hard, and I think, *Wow, that's how I like to wake up!*

But then I feel like she's actually blowing air down my throat? *What?*

I want to say something, but I can't really move or form words. Instead, I just groan and whimper like a kicked dog.

Then I throw up. On Cherie. And I realize I am lying on my back at the bottom of the pool and there is blood. All. Over. Me.

"What the fuck!" Cherie is yelling at me.

I don't understand what's happening. She's yelling at me and is covered in my barf. And my blood, I guess?

I want to ask, *What is going on?* But no words come out my mouth, only a groaning sound like a wounded dog who's been hit by a car.

The more she yells, the more I wail. She gets up and runs out of the pool. I follow her with my head, but then it feels like the whole world is spinning spinning spinning, and it gets dark and hazy again. Where are the others? Where are Alex and Bobby and what's-his-name? Where—

When I wake up again, there is somebody in a uniform strapping something around my neck.

He sees me looking at him and he says, "Hey, buddy, glad to see you waking up. How do you feel?"

I groan, but no words come out. My eyes wander, and I see Cherie dressed in a robe. She does not look happy. The guy focuses my attention.

"Hey. Hey." He snaps in my face. "Do you know your name?"

"What? Do I know my name? My name is . . . What?"

"Do you know where you are?"

I just look back at him like he's an idiot. "In bed?"

"Okay, okay, no worries. Seems you tried to go swimming without any water in the pool. Look before you leap, I always say. Are your parents home?"

He turns and asks Cherie, but she says that I don't live here, so she doesn't know. He notices I am wearing a metal bracelet that has my emergency contact info on it.

"Never mind," he says. "I got you . . . Gio. We're gonna take you to the ER to check you out, and I'm gonna call your parents so they can meet you there. You're gonna be all right, buddy, don't worry. You got knocked out pretty good, but I don't think your neck is broken. I'm not gonna lie, though. Life's gonna suck for a while."

Yes, it did.

So what happened when I reached my triumphant peak was my new wheels caught on the coping and I fell face-first from ten feet up onto the cement bottom of the pool, cracking my head, breaking my nose, and knocking out my two front teeth. My "friends" panicked and freaked the fuck out and took off.

That left Cherie, who thought I wasn't breathing, to give me mouth-to-mouth, resulting in her getting puked on. My parents freaked, and in my concussed haze, I might've mentioned I'd been skating in the pool, and my mom might've said something like "My son is the Pool Bandit?!" And I might have said, "Not just me, but Alex and Skeezer and Bobby." It was all a blur.

Cherie got in trouble and so did we, and not only were my friends not talking to me but we all had to do two hundred hours of community service and clean all three pools that we'd damaged and apologize in person to the families we had taken advantage of. No one would talk to me. I wasn't sure if it was 'cause I told on them or 'cause they felt bad for leaving me and didn't know what to say.

Things just got more awkward as the time passed. Needless to say, my parents took away my board and I was grounded for life—only to be let out for community service. The rest of the Bandits worked off their hours on different gigs, so I didn't see them. And Cherie never looked at me again.

The rest of the summer sucked ass. I was confined to my room for a few weeks and had to get fake front teeth (which my dad says I will be paying off for the rest of my life) and get my nose straightened. My sister loved to shake her head at me, like, *I knew this was coming.* But even she felt sorry for me after a while.

One day, she bought me a copy of the new *SkateBoarder* because it showed the plans for the first skate park in the South Bay. Skateboard World was only ten minutes from our house and even had bowls shaped like pools. "That's gonna be the future," Lisa said. "You won't have to drain anyone's pools anymore."

I didn't care.

It wasn't till fall semester, when I was back in school, that I almost ran into Skeezer, Alex, and Bobby in the bathroom between periods. We had no classes together. I was in the stall, doing my business, when they walked in talking about a secret underground pipe that ran the length of the LA airport. It had been discovered by one of the Dogtown Boyz and had miles of perfect skateable banks. You had to enter through one of the drainage ditches off the main highway, but once you were in, you could skate for hours with no hassles.

Alex was pushing them to go, but Bobby was reluctant.

"What're you, scared?" Alex said.

Skeezer told him to shut up. Then he said if they were gonna do anything, they should bring me.

"Gio?" said Alex. My name hung in the air for a minute. Then he said, "You think?"

I was kind of taken aback. What was there to think about? I was about to bang the door open and say, *Fuck yeah, motherfuckers, let's do this! We'll shred those pipes!*

Instead, I sat there and listened as Bobby described the pipes in more detail. He'd heard about it from his brother, Rory, who was now a skater too. Not only that, but apparently, he was buddies with Alva, who he'd met skating . . . in a pool.

I guess we'd made it cool enough?

They headed out the door, still arguing about whether to go or not, and the room went quiet. I sat there thinking maybe I could go scope the pipes out for them, just like the old days.

Then I imagined me showing them what I found. We'd climb down some sewer drain together while the traffic and 747s roared overhead. The deeper we got, the quieter it'd seem. Then we'd come out into some huge-ass pipe that was, like, thirty feet tall. Our headlamps would catch the top of the tube arching high over us like a cathedral. We'd look at each other and laugh. Our own Disneyland.

Alex would nudge me on the shoulder and say, "Good find." Bobby and Skeezer would whoop and holler just to hear the echoes of their own voice. Then I'd kick off.

Follow me! We'd all skate in a row, weaving like a snake for miles, going up and down back and forth as we headed deeper and deeper into what seemed like a perfect endless wave.

I thought about running out after them to catch up. But the bell was about to ring, and what would I say anyways? Instead, I dug that *SkateBoarder* magazine out of my backpack and flipped to the pages about the coming wave of skate parks being built around the southland. Skatopia, The Pipeline, Concrete Wave, Big O . . . They looked pretty rad. But they'd charge a fee to get in and make you wear some sucky helmets and kneepads and there would be rules to follow and lines to drop into a bowl and parents waiting at the snack bar . . . It wasn't the same. It wasn't like sleeping in a stranger's pool or being chased down by cops or stealing wood to build a ramp.

Fuck that. I tossed the mag and made plans to do some recon for the pipes underneath the airport. The Pool Bandits would expect nothing less.

After school, I was feeling a little less certain. I had no board and no idea how to find the pipes. I needed the guys, but maybe they didn't need me anymore.

I was standing in the parking lot staring off into the distance when I felt a shove from behind.

It was Alex. We stood there awkwardly eyeing each other. "You done with your service hours?" he asked.

I nodded. "You?"

"Yeah . . ." He looked at his feet, then back up at me. I could see him thinking, but neither of us knew what to say.

I cleared my throat and said, "My mom's been talking to my dad about maybe giving me back my board next month . . . but only if I promise to keep my head on straight. Whatever that means."

He kind of smirked and looked away, nodding. I'd heard his old man had sold his board to a neighborhood kid, but Alex just waited a bit and bought it back.

"Then you better keep it on straight," he said.

He turned and started walking away. But he glanced back over his shoulder, just for a second. And that's when I saw it: a glint of possibility in his eye.

I knew we were back on.

We Are Looking for Home
by A.S. King

We start in the garden. Of course. We start with our snowsuits on. Numb cheeks. Snot frozen to the ends of our noses. We start dumb, like everybody else. We start hungry. We don't know how to do what we do, but we do it anyway.

Get up for school / work / eat breakfast.

Brush teeth / clip toenails / comb hair.

Build snow sculptures / fashion ice battles / hot cocoa by the fire.

We do it all anyway.

These are the best years of our life. We go to school and learn things we will forget. We have accumulated trillions of memories between us. Amassed tragedies. Gathered all kinds of matter. Humans collect everything. We collect galaxies of information. We collect photographs. We collect the right thing to do in any situation. We collect the wrong things to do too. We are curators of joy and misery. We collect ourselves. We are dangerous.

The only humans who aren't dangerous are the ones who are looking for home. No one can be dangerous when looking for home. Or at least, it's not a wise approach. Home is a big deal—nobody can find it.

Jasper Miller got close once. Brought the photograph to class and showed us. Ninth grade.

"It's home," he said.

The picture was of cat litter. There was some cat shit in the litter. We mocked him for being so bad at humor / for being morose / for being cynical. We mocked him for his pimples and greasy hair. We were unstable compounds jammed into a test tube. We bubbled out and overflowed into Jasper Miller every one of our fears. For any of us, home could be cat shit. We just didn't like to think about it.

Jasper Miller didn't talk to us for a year after that. He learned to live without us. He pretended to be fine with it.

Almost everyone pretends.

That's why we can't find home.

When the world fell apart, it wasn't the biology that started it. Nothing to do with atoms or chemistry. Nothing to do with our pinkie fingers getting smaller. Nothing to do with the climate. It was psychology that ended us—poked holes in our brains until we couldn't function with each other / without each other.

We are a team now / they ruined us / they salvaged us / we stick together.

We don't care about home / we have too much work to do to worry about dumb things like home.

We are afraid to be alone.

· · · · · · · · · · · ·

Jasper Miller lives in the basement. "I need the cold," he says.

Jasper is a fantastic dancer. Jasper suffers from anxiety. Jasper suffers from imposter syndrome. Jasper suffers from being Jasper. "Staying warm keeps my mind off of everything else," he says. He does three pirouettes and then sits on the floor to stretch his hamstrings.

Jasper Miller wants to know what it's like to have friends.

We read him page one of the *us* handbook.

What's most important is being liked and popular.

Every time we read it, Jasper says, "Sounds like bullshit to me."

We shiver. Jasper is the only *we* that can *me*.

He is a *he* and not an *us* and, while *he* is part of our *we, we* are never our own. Jasper is. We think it's because of how he can't see how great he is on account of him having low self-esteem. Probably something to do with how we shunned him that one time freshman year. We build him up every day when we see him in the halls.

"You rock, Jasper."

"You're doing great, man!"

"Keep it up!"

We check on him a lot. We tell him that tomorrow is always a new day.

We worry: How can we find home if we are unliked and unpopular? We try not to hate Jasper Miller.

. . . .

We understand balance, which seems weird because we are teenagers and people say teenagers don't understand anything.

Last week, upon learning there are approximately three hundred million guns in America, we decided to balance that with three hundred million things of the opposite nature. Jasper Miller told us that if guns represent death, which is their only purpose, then we needed to balance them with something that represents life.

We called out ideas.

"Butterflies!"

"Oak trees!"

"Birds!"

"Babies!"

There were forty million ideas. We chose butterflies. For every gun in America, we matched a butterfly to counter it. Sometimes our ideas are good and proper. We have the best intentions. We start in the garden. We understand balance. We are oak trees / butterflies. Forty million acorns. Forty million pupae. Forty million eggs. Forty million zygotes.

Let us back up. We know we're confusing / always changing our minds.

We start in the garden—our mother's wombs / enemy territory. It's no wonder we can't find home.

We do not understand balance.

Jasper Miller says, "Come over for hot chocolate and a movie!"

We say, "That isn't a fair trade."

Jasper says, "My mom says you're entirely welcome. Right, Mom?"

Jasper's mother can't be seen by us nor heard. We aren't even sure if she's real. We once talked behind Jasper's back and decided that she probably isn't. Maybe this is why Jasper has such low self-esteem. He lies a mother into being.

We say, "Jasper, why can't you see how great you are?"

"Please come in. Leave your shoes by the door," Jasper Miller says.

Can't you see he's a control freak? It's infuriating how he can't see it.

Jasper Miller works every day inside of himself. He is building home. He started small, and it grew from there / a room / a house / a village / a town / a city / a whole fucking world. We don't understand why he would do this.

"I'm staying busy. It's better for me this way," he says.

He has built a church. It is the Church of Jasper Miller. It is the church where no one worships because Jasper Miller has disallowed worship. "Plus," he says, "it's not like I'm anything special."

He has no idea how much we covet his *I'm*. He is clearly some kind of god / will never accept that / is a common brown-nose / what a jerk.

We are looking for home, and we start in the garden. Soil is where to look if you want to start a thing. We want to plant Jasper Miller and see if he can grow big enough to make us all *me*. Instead, he grows apartment blocks inside himself for us. He cares that much / feels terrible about the whole thing.

We try so hard to be worthy of Jasper Miller's rent-free tenements—stacked up like shoe boxes in a basement—nobody knows what we'll be used for, but one day we will find out. We try to have a good attitude, but inevitably, we aim low.

Our parents tell us it will pass.

"It's hormones."

"It's just your age."

"Growing up is hard."

Jasper tells us not to listen. He says we are as varied as the stars and our problems are valid and not related to our age. We tell Jasper Miller that we don't have any problems.

"Can't you see how beautiful it is to be honest?" he asks.

We laugh at him.

He whispers, "Are you even listening to me?"

He walks into his bedroom and slams the door. We are left standing in his yard, staring at the garden. Soil is where to look if you want to start a thing. We want to plant Jasper Miller and see if he can grow big enough to make us all *me*.

. . . .

Jasper Miller's house is a brown-siding-covered split level with yellow faux shutters. In summer, his front yard is always perfectly green. His backyard contains a vegetable garden and an out-of-ground swimming pool. In winter, the pool is empty, and sometimes Jasper hides in it.

He hides from us. We are always doing things that make him mad. We are always looking for home.

We're having a snowball fight again.

We started in the garden / now we are pummeling Jasper Miller, who cowers in the shell of his swimming pool under a sky-blue tarp, with forty million snowballs. He is no match for us. We are a collection of weight lifters / basketball players / boxers / field hockey players / future physicists / really nice kids / girls who beat you up after school / valedictorians / majorettes / none of us believe Jasper Miller has parents.

"Stop that!" someone says, but we can't see who.

"If you don't stop, I'll call the police!" a male voice says. We can't see him either.

"We don't listen to invisible people!" we say.

Soon we hear police sirens. The sky opens and there is sleet. We run to our homes. We are *we*, but we live in individual homes and are driven to school in individual cars. We communicate through social media servers that reinforce every bad thing we ever think. Tomorrow is a school day. The snowball fights are over. We eat dinner and watch TV. We forget to study for a test. We remember every single capital of every single European country. We are not allowed to read any book with the word "fuck" in it. Even though we have said the word "fuck" 1,800,000,000,000 times. We are assumed stupid until proven worth listening to. We are rushed, constantly, by bells / schedules / commercials / what to buy next. It's usually sex.

The sleet hits our bedroom windows as we sleep.

We dream of money.

. . . .

Monday. Jasper Miller gives a springtime homeroom sermon. He says:

"This morning I overheard a parent in the school parking lot saying, 'You make our family look bad!' It was one of your parents. And I'm sorry."

"What are you sorry for, Jasper?" we ask.

"I have failed all of you."

"We threw forty million snowballs at you. We are ashamed."

Jasper says, "You have nothing to be ashamed about. Snowball fights are fun."

This leaves the space very quiet. We don't feel like anyone wants us to have fun. Not even ourselves.

This is why we worship at the Church of Jasper Miller. We are cowering in a science wing closet. We are cowering at our part-time jobs. Four-to-eight shifts that have us on our school laptops until midnight. Forty million butterflies set aside for the love of violence / laughing to prove that we are living the best years of our lives—just like they said. Jasper Miller wants us to have fun. In the backyards of the tenements inside his chest, he is building forty million playgrounds. He plans a clubhouse for the next cold winter, full of arcade games and the world's biggest cineplex.

Tuesday. Today Jasper Miller brings a yo-yo. He tells us it is home.

We stopped listening to Jasper Miller a long time ago. The boy is a flake. A real flower. Someone ought to give him a bus ticket to wherever they care about a guy like that. Everybody knows fun is for little kids and kittens. Our parents tell us he makes his family look bad. We decide his church should be boarded up and burned. We do it in our minds because that's the only place the Church of Jasper Miller lives.

It starts in the garden / matches / no rain for weeks.

It starts with skin greasy from grass mowing and eating too many oven French fries while our parents are still at work.

It starts with a girl named Lena. A wrong number. Jasper replies: *Sorry, but you have the wrong number.* She replies: *Maybe this is fate. God wants us to meet.*

Jasper Miller shows it to us at lunch and says, "This could be a clue."

Wednesday. Jasper brings a piece of the Berlin Wall. He says it is the home of sand and molecules of spray paint. It is the home of keeping us in line. The home of order.

"We like order!" we say to Jasper Miller.

"As long as you don't like it too much," he says.

We say, "Do you have to argue with everything all the time?"

Jasper shows us the new building inside his chest. It's less like a brick tenement and more like a condo skyscraper—something from Dubai or Hong Kong—with balconies and barstools and bathtubs.

"How will you decide who lives there and who lives in these old dumps?" we ask.

"Dumps?" Jasper asks.

"We don't have balconies," we say.

"But you have home."

Jasper says this, but we don't believe him.

Thursday. Jasper brings twenty million pieces of sandpaper and asks us to pair up and share.

"Start smoothing things out," he says. "Trust me. It's such a nice feeling."

We take the sandpaper and rub it on our arms and on the arms of people next to us.

"Not on your partner!" Jasper says.

"We are looking for home," we say.

"Stop saying that," Jasper says.

Jasper doesn't come in on Friday. We meet at lunch and try to figure out what Jasper would have brought for us if he were there.

Forty million tiny guitars.

Forty million seagulls.

Forty million gift cards from that tattoo place in town.

We call out the designs we would get.

"A lion!"

"An umbrella!"

"A hunk of cheese!"

Jasper isn't around on the weekend. Or the next week. Or the next.

He sends word. *I am tired of being me. I need a break.*

We live in Jasper's chest / we have a balcony / we have barstools / seesaws / swing sets. We live in his *I'm* / in his *he*. We hate him so much we taste blood—his blood—it's what happens when we twist the spigot.

· · · · · · · · · · · ·

Lena comes by train from Philadelphia. She is tall and stick thin but not in a bad way. We like her. We don't want to. She eats three fried ice cream sandwiches from the taco truck faster than we've ever seen anyone do that.

"How can you do that and not get brain freeze?" we ask.

"Magic, I guess," Lena answers.

"Don't you care if you get fat?" we ask.

"No?" she answers, turning the inflection up at the end, like the tip of her nose.

Jasper comes over then, and he's shy around her. We don't understand this. We would do it totally different if we had a girl like that. We are forty million pretenders. Last year, we pretended to love a girl like Lena until she broke up with us because she didn't like how we never held her hand but kept telling her that we are very good at sex. She didn't like how on the last day of baseball, we followed that queer kid down the hall and pretended to beat him with our bats. We don't care what she thinks. We fear nothing.

"Where are you going, Jasper?" we yell as he and Lena head toward the park.

"I won't be in school again tomorrow," Jasper answers.

He and Lena walk close to each other. They don't hold hands. But there is something between them. She likes him. As she talks, her hands move, and she's excited to let him in on a secret. Jasper is transfixed. It's as if no one else matters to the two of them. It's infuriating.

We follow them to the park. But then we are called for dinner. All of us have eaten too much taco truck food, so we're not hungry. Our parents ask, "Don't you like the food?" / "Is someone bullying you at school?" / "Are you suffering from depression?"

The next day we cower in our chemistry lab closet, lit by the glow of our phone screens, writing to our parents to let them know this time's for real. This is the worst time to be us. *Us.* We can't write to our parents the way Jasper does. When we try to type *I*, our phone autocorrects to *We*. *We love you*, we write. *We're sorry for everything we've done wrong*. We didn't do our chemistry homework, for one thing, and even though we know what's happening outside of the closet, we're grateful to not be found out.

Jasper Miller once told us homework is important. But he's a jerk, right? Thinks he's so smart, doesn't he? Well, where is he today?

We pass around vapes in the closet and someone coughs and the teacher tells us to stay quiet.

The cops come and arrest the guy. He didn't even get one shot off. What a loser.

School is dismissed, and we go home to our parents, who demand to know what we were referring to when we said we were sorry for the things we did wrong. We can't answer / we don't know / we feel suddenly and overwhelmingly tired.

We sleep from Friday night to Monday morning.

. . . .

We start in the foyer of the school—right next to the main office. At the end of the hall is the guidance office, which has a mural on the walls around it of Snoopy and Woodstock and Charlie Brown. We think someone painted it in 1985. It shows. Snoopy's white coat has significant traces of age. His perky ear looks disconnected from his head.

We remove our ears from our heads.

We walk the halls and don't hear a thing.

We follow the queer kid to his locker. We whisper, "You should kill yourself," and walk on to lunch. We consider eating our own ears. This way we won't ever have to hear how awful we are.

We are called to the vice principal's office after eighth period. We wait next to three desks full of busy secretaries. We stare at the stickers on the backs of their monitors. One says YOU ARE WORTH A MILLION

OCEANS. We laugh. We are forty million oceans who can't find home /
soon, the things our parents say to us will not matter.

The vice principal scoots us into his little office.

"Did you say dumb shit to the queer kid?" he asks.

"We didn't even know there was a queer kid."

We are forty million liars. We are, some of us, queer kids ourselves.
This morning we watched thirty-four TikToks about how to be better at
making friends. This morning we Googled how to tell if our boyfriend
is cheating on us. This morning we found beer cans in our recycling /
the smell of red wine permeating our dishwashers. This morning we
pledged allegiance to what everyone thinks of us.

We fill every pore of the vice principal's office. When he sweats
during baseball practice after school, he is sweating us. We are snot on
the end of his nose. We are foul balls / home runs / bullies.

We are sorry.

We don't know how to make friends.

"I can't give you detention," the vice principal says.

We smile.

"Just go easy on that kid, okay? And try to use deodorant." He
pinches his face in disgust.

"We didn't even know there was a queer kid," we say again. When
we say it, he makes an expression like our breath reeks.

Jasper Miller is outside the office when we exit. He says, "Hey."

We say, "Hi."

He says, "Want to come to my house after school to study?"

We say, "Why do you always have to be so nice?"

Jasper shrugs.

We spend the rest of the day sniffing our own armpits and not talking to the girls we like, just in case.

No one mentions the guy who got arrested on Friday / how we texted our parents love letters / how we could have all been murdered / how this might affect our future prospects. There are two policemen in the hallways whenever the bell rings. They smile as if they know a secret that we don't.

We pretend we're not bothered by it / sign up for the SAT exam. We ask one another to the prom / rent tuxedos because we're feeling lucky. We don't know what maturity is / we cry at the mere thought of an animal suffering / we gossip so brutal it breaks skin / this week they banned a book at our school about lesbians who have periods.

We are your trash can—we are your mirror. Home is never going to find us if we all can't agree to be nice. It has to be a unanimous vote.

Later that day, Jasper Miller offers, as standard, to his forty million tenants, full cable TV, internet, and all utilities paid.

He thinks he's so special.

It's disgusting.

. . . .

Lena comes to see Jasper Miller every weekend.

"Did you fuck her yet?" we ask him as he walks home from the bus station late Sunday afternoon.

"Shut up," he says.

There are forty million giggles. "Jasper is afraid!" we taunt.

"I'm not afraid," Jasper says. "I'm mature. There's a difference."

"We aren't here for a sermon from a virgin," we say.

"Virgins can't teach us a damn thing," we say.

Jasper stays quiet. He looks fine. Our taunts do nothing to him. We move on to the park and find two middle schoolers. We tell them they're gay and make kissing noises. We try to not swear in front of the littler kids playing there. We're not monsters. We remember being little. It was mostly nice.

Jasper keeps to himself now, for the most part. He attends the ceramics club because Lena loves pottery. "It's very relaxing," Jasper says. "Do any of you want to try?"

"What happened to you loving dancing?" we ask.

Jasper shrugs.

We climb inside his chest, into our living rooms, and watch TV while Jasper throws pots on a wheel and listens to grunge music from the 1990s because the pottery teacher is a Gen-X failure. You know what they say about teachers.

We don't trust our parents / we believe everything they say. Inside of us is a divide—a fault we fall into every day. We believe our mothers are crazy / they had it coming / best mom in the world. We believe our fathers are saints because they say so. We pledge allegiance to the flag of whatever keeps us safe from ridicule.

It changes / we are cunning / we run three-minute miles—usually toward Jasper Miller and his girlfriend, Lena. On the way we lean into the weird girl with the purple hair at her locker and say, "You should kill yourself."

We land in the vice principal's office again. We see the stickers on the backs of the secretaries' computer monitors. YOU ARE WORTH A MILLION OCEANS is so stupid. No one can be both the ocean and worth a million of themselves. *You* is a lie. There is no *you*.

The vice principal greets us with forty million ice creams.

The vice principal greets us with forty million stickers that read, BE KIND!

. . . .

Now Jasper Miller and Lena Brain Freeze hold hands all the time. They walk home from school with the queer kid and the purple-haired weird girl. There are three others who follow them, pretending they have found home. Losers.

We follow them through the park. We've divided ourselves into teams—whoever finds home first gets to kiss us. Not just a peck on the lips either.

None of us can find it. We watch Jasper and Lena and the five others walk up the steps and out of the park. We call our parents and frantically arrange a sleepover. When we lie down to sleep, we hold hands to feel safe. We speak many things in the dark. We speak of fear. We speak of love. We pledge allegiance to the flag of whatever gets us out of this. We text each other all night long. We are afraid to sleep.

We wake up to forty million stacks of pancakes and forty million servings of link sausage.

We take a walk and notice buds opening on the trees. We love spring because spring means the end of winter. In six months, we will celebrate the end of summer too. We are on a water wheel of endings. Get the test done / get the good grade / get the shift punched out / wash the dishes / take out the trash. Endings are all trash. After something is over, all that's left is trash.

We start in the garden, no snot, no snowballs, no proof of breath. We are weeding a flower bed. There is a pile of mulch, a shovel, and a wheelbarrow. We are angry and tired. We can't wait for summer vacation.

Jasper Miller and Lena Brain Freeze walk by holding hands. We yell, "Jasper!"

Jasper smiles and stops to talk. "The flower bed looks great!" he says.

"Thanks," we answer.

"What are you doing later? My parents are filling the pool, and I have to sit around and make sure there are no leaks."

"Leaks?" we say.

"I'll be there after two," Jasper says. "You're all welcome."

Sounds like he thinks he's some kind of expert.

He's already walking away from us. We kick over the wheelbarrow / walk toward the park / past the queer kid's house. When we get in front of it, we take the rainbow flag from the front pillar, pole and all, and parade up the street with it.

"What a liar," we say to each other, "trying to tell us that we're all welcome."

"Maybe he means it," we answer back. We look at the porches of the houses we walk by—decorated with signs or lights, or both. ALL ARE WELCOME. WE LOVE OUR HOME. There are pillows with our last name / zip code / dog's breed on it.

"What a shyster," we say.

A police car creeps down the road with its lights on. We continue our parade and wave the flag we stole from the queer kid's house. We hope the police are going to arrest Jasper Miller. No one should be so happy and welcoming to forty million strangers. No one should have a whole world inside of him / skyscraper condominiums / barstools / bathtubs / swing sets / us.

When the police car stops and the cop yells, "Hey! Stop!" we realize that *we* are why the police are here. We look at each other, panicked / drop the stolen flag. Ten million of us scatter. Ten million of us start to cry. Ten million of us say, "It's Jasper Miller's fault!" Ten million of us run straight for the police officer and tackle him.

We warned you we were dangerous.

. . . .

We would not be in this much trouble if we would have followed Jasper Miller's example. If the police ever asked him to stop, he would have stopped and probably offered the officer something nice to eat. Or a hug. Or a penthouse apartment—the ones with the extra-long balconies. Jasper Miller doesn't know what to say to us when he sees the policeman on the ground, out cold.

He checks the cop's pulse and breathing.

He finally says, "You can't keep doing this."

We plead. "Please forgive us!"

Jasper sighs. We all know Jasper can't walk away. We are inside of him. We are a terrible disease / forty million parasites.

"I trusted you," Jasper says, a gracious host.

"We thought it was the right thing to do!" we say.

"Bullshit," Jasper says.

We don't know what to do when home is mad at us. It feels desperate and pointless. We are not always strong enough to take it. Life shouldn't be / school shouldn't be / home shouldn't be a test of strength.

We are confused all the time / trying to be mature / acting like our parents.

Nothing makes sense unless we twist it into something ugly / unless we win.

. . . .

Jasper Miller is distributing eviction notices. We vow to fight. He can't just toss us out like this. We trusted him. What an asshole. We record ourselves talking shit about him and send the recording to his ears. He hears us all day long. But he always did. Everyone hears us all day long.

We are everyone. We are the worst anyone ever expected, and we show the fuck up for work.

We pledge allegiance to the flag of making you doubt everything about yourself.

. . . .

Jasper Miller and Lena got pretend married at the campsite where they went canoeing over the weekend. Jasper said he gave Lena a ring made out of braided wildflower stems. She gave him a ring made of a piece of plastic she found on her suburban Philly road.

"So—you're a married man?" we ask Jasper.

"Yes." Jasper smiles. We can see that he knows everything now. We were always told that growing up allows a man to see everything. Marriage is the shortcut.

"Where is your bride?" we ask.

"Back in Philadelphia," Jasper says. "I will have to wait for her to come visit before I see her again."

We console Jasper. Our hugs press the air out of his lungs. We ask, "Why don't you go to Philadelphia?"

"I can't."

We know, deep down, that shortcuts have consequences. Jasper Miller is no man to pair something as precious as *I* with a tragic word like "can't."

We know Jasper and Lena aren't really married, they are just play-acting like kindergarten playgrounds. We remember kindergarten. We remember playing Hide in the Bathroom with Mrs. Lutz with the lights off. We remember laughing at Jasper because he had to stand behind the toilet for all of us to fit. We called him Toilet Head for about a week.

The eleventh-grade marriage of Toilet Head and Brain Freeze: because in kindergarten we were all too busy hiding in the bathroom. Pussies.

. . . .

We leave Jasper Miller slowly. We ooze out in ear wax and tears. We trickle through the sewers and back to our own predicament.

No one will want us now.

No one as kind and welcoming as Jasper.

We keep trying to get our keys back. Some of us decide to squat. We take drastic measures. "Jasper, your dick is so small! Lena thinks you smell bad! You will never grow up!"

None of it works.

"No one will ever like you!" Forty million butterflies arrive to balance us. We lunge at them, but they are not as easy to tackle as police officers.

"You should kill yourself." Forty million butterflies attack us with mirrors. We are forced to look at ourselves / see how terrible we are.

"We're sorry! We're sorry! We're sorry!"

We are alone.

We are desperate to start again.

. . . .

We start in the garden. Of course. We start with our swimsuits on. Numb cheeks. Goggles on the bridges of our noses. We start dumb, like everybody else. We start hungry. We don't know how to do what we do but we do it anyway.

We will grow into adults who don't know how to apologize / adults disconnected from reality as a form of self-preservation. We will crawl into anyplace that feels like home.

We inhabit whole families, whole communities. We pledge allegiance to the shit we always heard about you. (There is no you.) We aren't sorry. We aren't here. We aren't even real. We are the human soundtrack / bypassed the speakers / went directly to the source / your head.

Our home is you.

(Our home is you.)

. . . .

Jasper Miller and Lena Brain Freeze broke up in summer.

"It wasn't anyone's fault," Jasper says. "These things happen."

"We are sorry," we say.

"It's okay, Jasper," we say.

"Is there anything we can do?"

Get up for school / work / eat breakfast.

Brush teeth / clip toenails / comb hair.

Fall in love / break up / despair.

Jasper Miller's self-esteem ruined it. Lena tells her friends in Philadelphia about how Jasper is not ready for love.

"He's so charming and sweet," she says. "He offers help to anyone who needs it."

"Well then, what happened?" we ask.

"He was so concerned with everyone liking him, it didn't matter that I did," Lena says.

"That's sad," we say / we order catering for forty million.

Home is cat shit / we are happy when others fail / there will be a party tonight.

. . . .

Jasper Miller starts in the garden. Of course. It's where he works out his pain and loneliness. His father told him as they walked the bike trail last weekend that learning how to be alone is an important life skill.

"That's terrifying," Jasper said.

"Your generation doesn't . . ."

Jasper goes to the garden without his father. There is no age requirement for being lonely and it sucking.

We try to console him, but he yells at us / calls us ungrateful / we connect to the internet / watch nine videos about how to please our girlfriend / Google *how to stop being jealous of a friend*. We throw eggs at the queer kid's front door. Nothing fills the hole. Everything fills the hole. Everything is the queer kid's front door. We are the queer kid's front door.

Jasper calls Lena.

"I miss you," he says.

"I miss you too," she answers.

The exhale causes gale-force wind. It pulls pieces of us away from ourselves.

We are skin and dust and strands of hair / a funnel of opposing ideas / we are banished from Jasper's internal village. We will never forgive him. He will always win. We will never find home.

"Can I come see you?" Jasper says.

"Yes!" Lena says.

Jasper looks at his watch. "I can be there by seven, I think."

Lena starts to cry.

"Why are you crying?" Jasper Miller asks.

"I think I love you."

We crawl back into Jasper's housing development through the

unlocked windows. We teem through the stairwells and ventilation and up through the balcony railings. Forty million evictees waiting for love, just once to feel tenderness.

"I think I love you too," Jasper says.

We are suspended in space—a nothingness we weren't expecting.

We go to the garden.

We are looking for home.

We are afraid to be alone.

A Recording for Carole Before It All Goes
by Jason Reynolds

Your name. Carole. Care. Roll. My name is Carroll too. Just like yours, Grandma. But with two *r*s and two *l*s and no *e*. I was named after you. By your daughter, my mother.

Your daughter, my mother's, name. Christina. Chris. Tina.

Your son, my uncle's, name. Calamity. Cuh. Lamb. It. Ee. You call him Citty. He's your first child. You named him after what you thought he'd be because you were only fifteen when you gave birth to him. Only fifteen when everyone told you your life was ruined. That the baby in your arms would wash your wishes away. Turns out, he's the sweetest. And we all know he's your favorite of the two.

Your dog's name. Cangaroo. Canga. Roo. He's a mutt but we think he's a mix of boxer and Great Dane. A dog-faced pony. You think he looks just like your dead husband. The grandfather I never met.

Cangaroo sleeps in the bed with you every night. You feed him scrambled eggs every morning. Chicken breast in the evening. I named Cangaroo "Kangaroo" when you first got him from the pound. When I told you I wanted to name him that, you said it was fine as long as we spell it with a *C*.

You love *C*s because they have no hard edges, and to you, hard edges have the potential to make boxes. And you don't do boxes. *They either preserve or they imprison, and I want neither. Let me wither away freely,* you'd say. However, circles you don't mind. You love to see Cangaroo run around and around and around, every time you come home. I don't remember why I chose that name. Maybe because he was hoppy when you got him. He was still young then. He's twelve now, which makes him exactly the same age as you in human years. So the running in circles, though it still happens, has slowed down some. It's more like a saunter. But the excitement to be with you hasn't dwindled at all. His tail still whips anything sad out of the way and clears a path for slobbery kisses. My father calls Cangaroo your third child. You call him your fourth. After my father.

My father's name. Martin. Mar. Tin. You love him. But when Christina introduced him to you, you were upset his name didn't begin with *C*. You thought it might've been a sign he wasn't the one. That's what you used to tell me. But then you found out his middle name was Curtis and that was enough.

You call him Curtis. Cur. Tis. And he lets you. Because he loves you too. In the spring and summer he comes over and cuts your grass without asking. He also trims your hedges. In the fall, he rakes your leaves. And this time of year, he shovels your driveway. You always offer him ten dollars. He never takes it. He likes to kiss you on the cheek. You like when he does it. He also takes you to your doctor's appointments: the foot doctor, the belly doctor, the cancer doctor.

You have terrible feet from forty years of wearing high heels and walking back and forth across your classroom, and up and down the halls of the high school you worked at. Your feet look like arrowheads. Don't be alarmed.

Your stomach is glitchy. If you eat salad, you won't poop for a week. You love salad. But you hate tomatoes. If you eat anything rich—butter, cream, cheese, oil—you'll have diarrhea, and you move too slow these days to make it to the toilet. Everything causes gas. Anger. Joy. Anxiety. Excitement. Curtis tells Christina that the doctor says your bad stomach just comes with age. *Her stomach might be bad, but her gut is good,* Christina said.

The cancer doctor says you still don't have cancer. Again. It's important that you know you've had it once. I think I was six, so maybe eight or nine years ago. You don't have breasts. You hate the word "breasts," and prefer the word "boobs," but Christina makes me say "breasts." You no longer have any. They were removed when you had cancer. You also don't have hair. It never grew back after the treatment. But you have the best selection of wigs I've ever seen. Short red ones. Puffy black ones. Spiky gray ones. Long silky ones. You even have one that's pre-braided. That one might be my favorite. It might be yours too. Citty has bought them all for you.

Curtis doesn't take you to the brain doctor. Those appointments are for Christina and Citty. Christina would take you by herself, but the truth is she hates receiving bad news about you alone. When Citty can't make it, when he's busy with his acting, she takes me.

Citty is an actor. For a living. Sometimes you will see him on television, and when you do, he'll be acting like someone else. But around you, he will never act like anyone else besides Calamity Brown, your first and favorite born.

Your last name is Brown. Nothing interesting about that, but I guess it's important to note in case someone ever asks.

Christina is a tattoo artist. She owns her own shop, which is why she has flexibility when it comes to taking you to the brain doctor. My job is to help where I can, even if that means passing her tissues at the doctor's office when you try to lighten the mood and crack jokes about whether or not you'll be lucky enough to forget your age or your weight or that "crusty-toed son of a bitch Marshall."

Mar. Shull. That is your husband's name. Was. The one that Cangaroo resembles. Maybe I should leave him out of this. But you loved him. You also hated him because he left you for some woman, you, Christina, Citty, and Curtis all call Little Miss Fill in the Blank. You say you know he stepped out on you because of the ugly scar across your stomach. That he couldn't bear the sight of it. The one left by Christina's birth. *I should've known then,* you always say, *she was born to make permanent marks.* You tell me all this whenever I sit with you and watch the stories.

You love the stories. You tell me there's nothing more entertaining than watching rich white people get messy. We dunk Oreos in apple juice when we watch and when you tell me all the things you tell me. And you tell me a lot. Because we're best friends. You even told me how you discovered Oreos would be good with apple juice. *What's not to like about chocolate-covered apples?*

I'm the one thing you tell the doctor you never want to forget.

We don't know how long it'll take the Alzheimer's to steal all your memories. But Dr. Drayton—that's your brain doctor's name—says physical activity three to four days a week can slow it down.

Your days are Monday, Tuesday, Thursday, Friday. You said you needed Wednesdays free for lunch dates with friends. You think I don't know about Christopher, the man you see on Wednesdays at the park. But I know about him. Because you told me he looks like an older version of Tupac, who you only know about from the crush Christina had on him when she was a teenager. *Posters on every wall in her room.* I don't bring Christopher up because it's weird to think about your grandma and her boyfriend who looks like Tupac kissing on a park bench. But Christina says he's nice. Has tattoos of daffodils up his arm. Her work. She's who introduced you.

Soon you'll have to tell me about him again. Or I'll have to tell you about him. Because you won't remember who Christopher is, and if you do, you won't remember the way to the park.

Saturday and Sunday are days off too. Saturday for rest. Sunday for Jesus, and family dinner.

But Monday, Tuesday, Thursday, and Friday, you box. You had a coach named Ricky, but once Dr. Drayton noticed your memory getting worse, he thought it would be best that we tighten your circle. So now Curtis is your boxing coach. No ring, no ropes. Just gloves and mitts in the living room. You blacked his eye once. Caught him with a right hook. Felt bad about it for a little while, then laughed with me about it over cookies and juice.

You like to flex your muscles. It reminds you that you're still powerful. You also like to dance. I mean that in the boxing way—light on your toes like how Cangaroo used to be—but also in the musical way.

Your favorite music is whatever Stevie Wonder makes. You love everything he's ever done, even the instrumental stuff about plants. Your favorite song is called "Visions." It goes like this: *I'm not one who make believes / I know that leaves are green / They only turn to brown when autumn comes around / I know just what I say / Today's not yesterday / And all things have an ending.* You love my singing voice. You say it reminds you of yours when you were younger. I hope this song, "Visions," reminds you about autumn and spring, especially when everything is cold and gray, like now. I hope it reminds you to water your plants, also a thing you do on Wednesdays. And if it doesn't, I will. Especially the rubber plant.

Your rubber plant's name. Carol. Care. Role. But with one *r* and one *l*. You named it after me. I bought it for you this time last year, as an early Christmas present. Christina and Citty got into a fight about whether or not you should name it. *It doesn't make sense to name a plant,* Christina said. *Of course it does. Everything deserves a name,* Citty said. *Not something that's guaranteed to die!* Christina said. And then you said, *Well, don't I have a name?*

When you decided to name it Carol, after me, Christina was even more upset. But I wasn't.

Carol is a year old and still healthy. To stay that way, it needs direct sunlight and generous water. Most important, Grandma, you have to talk to it. Tell it about the drama on the stories. Sing Stevie to it. Recite some of your unforgettables to it. Your name. Your age. Your birthday. Your address.

Your address. 2428 Seventeenth Street NW, Washington, DC. Your zip code is 20009. You've been living here for thirty years. Your house is red brick, but has a bright yellow door. Not sun yellow, or lemon yellow, or butter yellow. But highlighter yellow. Neon. Calamity chose the color, and Curtis painted it a while back to make sure you always know which house on the block is yours in case the numbers in your head aren't where they're supposed to be.

The day we knew things were off was last year on your seventieth birthday. Which reminds me, your birthday is July 18. It happened to land on a Sunday, which meant we could celebrate you at our usual family dinner. You still cooked because you love to cook. You also hate everyone else's cooking. We all showed up, ate everything, sang "Happy Birthday" to you, and presented you a cake. You wore a pink wig and refused to blow out the candles, afraid the hair would catch fire. When I asked you about how you'd make a wish, you told me you've been wishing your whole life, and they'd all come true, candles or no candles. Cake or no cake. Then Cangaroo started barking and scratching at the door. And even though we all know better than to try to walk him, because you don't let anyone walk your dog but you, Curtis told you he would do it. As a birthday favor. But you wouldn't allow it. Told him you'd throw cake at the back of his head, which was all he needed to hear to hand you the leash.

It's usually just a stroll up the block and back. Takes ten minutes, tops, unless Ms. Ferguson stops you to gossip about the neighborhood. Then it could take a little longer. But you were gone for almost twenty-five minutes before Christina poked her head out the door. You were nowhere to be found.

We split up, Christina, Citty, Curtis, and me. Citty went up the block. Christina went down. Curtis went toward Eighteenth Street, and I went toward Sixteenth. We called your name, asked neighbors who were outside tending to flower beds or fixing their cars if they'd seen an old lady in a pink wig and a dog-pony walk by. When I found you, you were standing in the doorway of a Metrobus, asking the driver how to get back to an address you couldn't remember. When I called out for you, you didn't turn around. But Cangaroo started to trot in circles. The second time I said your name, it caught. And you came toward me, hugged me with tears in your eyes.

You told me you didn't know where you were or how to get home. That somehow your house wasn't where you'd left it.

A month later, you'd had your first visit to the brain doctor. And Curtis had painted your front door. And you'd started boxing. And Christina had started looking for a house on your block for me, her, and Curtis to move into. In the meantime, Citty moved into your basement.

You also started telling me and Carol everything you remember.

And I began making these recordings for the moments you don't.

I love you, Grandma. I don't think you'll forget that. Even if you eventually forget me.

And if you ever forget your name—and I hope you never do, but if for some reason it's not where it's supposed to be, and you don't have this with you when someone asks it, remember, you had Christina tattoo it on your stomach.

Carole, right across that scar.

Sweet Everlasting

by M. T. Anderson

Shortly after the Fall of the Angels clattering down from Heaven to the lake of fire, or maybe after the Churning of the Sea of Milk, back when the world was just a soup of acids, humankind was created and immediately the demon Flaëlphagor hated them. He hated the way they walked around on two legs and reached for things in trees. He hated the shrieking noises they made when they were little, larval, screaming maggots—and he hated the honking noises they made when they were older and furry and wanted to declare love or war. He despised them for how short their lives were, how quickly they fell to aging and rot.

And as this filthy little race began to build their mud cities and dream they were kings of the world, the demon Flaëlphagor began a ghastly collection: His spirit drifted through history and picked through the humans as they lived their tiny lives and died; he sorted like a child browsing through a box of pretty rocks, and every time he came across a human who thought to themself, I wish this moment would last forever, *the demon snatched them up right then, froze them in time, and, hideously, gave them exactly what they asked for.*

. . . .

Raff, age seventeen, Lincoln, Massachusetts, 2021

Raff saw her first in the fifteenth century. That's where the Rise of the Modern World class started. She was a face in the corner of the screen, always beautiful, always in thought. She could have been one of the queens they were tested on, but there she was in his actual class, surrounded by black squares and the dull faces of other kids lit by their screens.

It was the pandemic that year, and they could not meet. All classes were remote.

Raff liked what she said when she turned on her mic and answered a question, even though he wasn't really paying attention to the class and so what she said was like, *Blah blah blah the Renaissance something something.* Her voice was beautiful through the mic and the app and the cable link and the speakers. She spoke softly, and the letters *t* and *p* when she said them clicked quietly in his headphones and made his scalp actually tickle.

He wished he could hear them at night, right in his ear, in the same way.

Finally, he told Buck to help him with courage, and Buck was like, "Screw it, just text her," and so Raff texted her, *Hey, I'm in your history class*, and then there was a day where she didn't respond and Raff sat tapping a pen on the countertop. "Stop tapping your pen," said his mom. "You're driving me crazy."

Then the girl texted back and was like, *Hey.*

He asked her for help on homework. It gave him an excuse to talk to her. He was pretty handsome, so she didn't need much of an excuse. Pretty soon they were texting back and forth all the time, even during class.

He couldn't wait to meet her in person, and he couldn't wait to actually touch her. He thought about her at night.

He started calling her his girlfriend even though they had never met.

So the snow came and went and finally that spring they had classes in person again and for the first time they were actually in the same room, and he saw how much taller he was than her. He felt like a man. He could tell she liked his height. He could tell they both wanted him to stoop down and kiss her.

But he didn't because it would be better for later that afternoon.

He was like, "I'll come over to your house after school," and she actually blushed a little and said, "Cool."

He thought maybe he was in love.

Riding in his mom's car with the windows open was great with the leaves green all around him—everything newborn, everything growing—and the air smelled sweet sometimes, like new grass. The air was swarming with possibility. Everything looked wet and welcoming.

He got to her house and was like, *I'm going to go in there and it's going to be just like a movie, we're going to not talk but just grab on to each other and start like kissing really hard and fall against the wall or maybe on the staircase.* But when she opened the door, he realized they'd basically never really even stood near each other and he didn't know what to say and so they ended up sitting on opposite sides of the sofa because they didn't really know each other at all. They had never even spoken alone in person except online. Now they talked about polite things, like history class and who they knew in common. They were like, "Yeah, Buck's a crazy f'ing kid. That kid is crazy."

Raff laughed, but he couldn't believe it was so awkward, sitting with her.

Then her dad came home and was like, "Hey, who's this?" and Raff told him, "Raphael, sir," and everything was very formal. They had a boring discussion about pandemic learning. Then her father said, "Well, Raff, you probably better be heading home," and so Raff somehow stupidly agreed and discovered that he was standing up and was shaking her hand—*shaking her hand!*—and walking out the door.

"God-f'ing-damn," he said to his steering wheel, and then he drove the two miles home. He parked and walked into the house and sat down on a chair and stood up and walked around the chair two times and sat down again.

Immediately, he texted her like, *Hey, that was weird*, and she agreed and they were both glad they admitted it, because it made them a team again.

He ate some old ribs for dinner and then he was texting her and he was like, *I want to see you again.* And she was like, *I wanna see YOU again*, and he was like, *I wanna see UUUUUU again*, and she was like, *Park at Craigie Circle. I'll meet you by the river.*

And he was like, *Holy shit*, and told his mom he was going over to Buck's and could he borrow the car? She said yes and he ran out to the driveway and backed the car out onto the street and loved the way it bounced once when it hit the pavement, like, *We're on an adventure now*, and he sped over to Craigie Circle and pulled over and there she was, sitting like a dream under a single streetlamp. Lit up like the main event.

So he went to her, and this time they didn't talk; they had that thing where they just started kissing. He felt her actual body under his hands—its weight, its solidity, its reality. It was no vision. It was not virtual. She filled the space between his arms. He said could they get on the ground, and she was like, "Yeah," and he laid her down behind the bench and put his arms around her again and their lips met again and he pulled her on top of him and her weight was upon him and he could smell the sweet scent of her, finally—finally—and then he was like, *Holy shit, I wish this moment could last forever.*

Their bodies were never found.

. . . .

At first, of course, there was the panic, because his body had locked and his face was against another face and there was not much air. He tried to struggle, but he could not struggle because time had stopped, except for his thinking, and so there was no motion possible. He tried to scream out to her for help, but his lips wouldn't work. They were just slathered onto hers and couldn't move. *She's got to notice I'm, like, having a fit or a seizure or something,* he thought, but then he saw there was a look in her eyes, some panic, and he realized she was feeling it too. He tried taking his arms from around her and they wouldn't move. The fingers of one hand had gone up the back of her hoodie and were on her smooth skin, but he could not pull that hand out. His arms were not clenched, but he did not have the power of motion, and so their limbs were stranded as if they were wood.

There still was a glimpse of something hot—because now he became very aware that her breasts were pressed against him, and they were also solid and real—but that didn't last very long because he was becoming aware that where they were lying, behind the bench, there was not much grass. It was mostly sand and pebbles, maybe a couple bottle caps with their sharp, serrated edges making rings in his back.

Then there was her weight. Over the years he would come to estimate that it was maybe 115 pounds, but of course he would never find out if he was right, because he never could ask her, though his mouth could not have been closer to hers.

The ground was not level. There were several patches of grass, yes, but also, as it happened, his head was slightly lower than his feet. The ground must dip down. Within an hour he was desperate to stretch his neck. It was kinked. His skull was lifted slightly off the dirt to reach her lips with his, and now its elevation was torture.

Every joint of her body dug into him.

They will come and save us, he thought after a couple of hours, but there was no one who could find that gemlike, dark blue roundel of time where he was trapped with her. Police walked over the grass and rubble where they had lain. He never knew it.

A day. His arms were in impossible postures, he now knew. Not like love, but some dumb play about love. Like a kid drawing porn with stick figures. The awkwardness of their legs was very confusing, and then all too clear.

He had no idea what she was thinking behind the mask of her face. It was not even an inch from him. He could see the down on her cheek. Her thoughts were locked behind that mouth clamped on his. He could not know whether she hated him. He wondered. He hated that he even had to think about what she was thinking. Sometimes, he knew he hated her. He could not push her away, but he hated her. He knew it was not her fault, but that didn't stop him some months from hating her. They both lay there, silently, and the weeks went on, and the years went on.

It has been almost five hundred and seventy-five years now. They are still locked together. There is nothing to discuss. They know each other intimately, but they do not know each other at all. They never will.

Raff has tried to tell himself stories to mitigate the boredom. He has played games (counting pebbles that press into his back; making up names for the bush he can see out of the corner of his eye). He cannot stand the scent of her. It is cheap and chemical. Smell it long enough, and it's nothing but a spray, a vapor. He has no dream or wish but freeing himself from her. He suspects she dreams the same of him.

Raff has now gone entirely mad, locked inside the prison of his body, clamped inside the bars of her bones.

When I look at them gleaming before me—young love, preserved forever—I touch the meniscus of time that encases them, and out of frozen silence, I hear the screaming of their thoughts.

It is not so different from a marriage, after all.

This is a fine part of my collection.

The Sultan of the Great Seljuq Empire (for a day and a half), age thirty-two, the City of Merv, 1063

Out in the city's great square, the people were calling for their sultan. Tuqshurmish tightened the sash around his chest; he was sultan now. His father was dead, his brothers defeated. The golden throne of the Great Seljuq Empire was his, after years of battle: burning cities, slaughtering warriors, riding at the head of armies across the plains.

He had killed his final brother the day before. It was illegal to shed the blood of a Seljuq prince—high sacrilege. So Tuqshurmish had had him garroted. Strangled from behind with a bowstring until his eyes bulged and he stopped kicking and collapsed on the dirt floor of their tent.

Years ago, Tuqshurmish and his father and his brothers and the swarms of their people had swept down out of the northern grasslands, driving herds of sheep before them. No one had believed they could defeat the great kingdoms of the desert: the Arabs, the Persians. The walled cities had sent forth their armies in bright armor, some riding on the backs of war elephants.

But elephants are slow, and hardly made for fighting in the desert. They fell in battle. Over many years, Tuqshurmish and his family had taken rich city after rich city. *They called us barbarians,* he thought; *now we live in their empty palaces, and their people bow before us. Their holy men pray each Friday for us and for our eternal reign.*

Now, as the crowds called for him outside, the new sultan checked the flare of his mustache and the lay of his robes of shining silk brocade. That morning he had been bathed by the girls of conquered realms and sprinkled with perfumes. He no longer had the dust and blood of battle on him. He was clean, trim, perfect. He went out to meet his people.

He passed through the ranks of spearmen and halberdiers and through the columns of sunlight. He strode out onto the balcony above the great square of the city. There were thousands assembled before him, and a cheer went up. Pigeons were startled from the minarets of mosques and spun through the sky and their shadows wheeled across the crowd like the motions of history and the sultan greeted his people for the first time, planning wars and invasions and expansions into new kingdoms; the sound of their acclamation was not simply a noise, it was a force in the air, a sensation all along his arms; it was the joy of rulership itself, solid and tangible. He thought of all the battles, all the executions, his transformation from sweaty shepherd boy to ruler of half the world, and he almost laughed at the people below him, he almost laughed with giddy shock at their subjugation—and as he raised his hand again and they roared up to him, his heart lifted like one of those pigeons above the square and he thought, *I wish this moment could last forever...*

At first he did not know that he had been snatched away from his palace. He was aware only that the sound of screaming no longer had contours or syllables. It was one massive, crashing drone that went on and on, a thousand notes all sung together.

He could not lower his arm. *What is this, then?* he thought imperiously, as if whatever stroke had frozen him would answer to his kingship. As if Sickness itself would bow its poxy spine before his majesty and back away, murmuring, *Sorry, my sultan. I am sorry.*

But the sensation of being pinned in place would not go away. *I am stricken!* he thought, and struggled to breathe, but could not. He could not even grip his own throat in panic. He found, though, that he did not need air. The only thing that moved in his body was thought. And so he stood with his arm raised, and thousands stood below him, their mouths open in shouts, their fists raised over their heads.

Mouths open, fists closed. All of this in praise of him. He looked out upon his people and felt their adoration in the sound that roared around him. Their love for him was almost stupid. They would not stop screaming. Proudly, he realized: they could not stop. They would sing his praises until the end of time.

If this is going to be my stance until the angels release me, he thought, *then I shall stand here before my people like a true sultan!* And he inhabited every inch of his body, which stood like a statue on the balcony. He did not stand like a creature caught in its shell, but inserted pride into that frozen, raised hand as if he were slipping on a glove: a hand within his hand. He felt the constant wave of roaring wash across his stranded, triumphant body. He looked out over the heads of those who loved him.

After a few days, he began to wish he had learned to read. The mosque on the other side of the square was illuminated with Arabic calligraphy interwound with ornate designs on tile and it would maybe stem the boredom if he could read the holy words of wisdom there. He wondered what it all said, and vowed to have a good talk with the wise men and the ulama when the angels released him from all this glory and he was standing back on Earth again. And when, frankly, this sound got quieter. It was hard to think with all the roaring.

And hard to stand with all those eyes on him all the time. Never blinking. He was always standing before the public. Always exposed to them. Their fists raised. Their mouths open.

He looked out at the crowd. There was time to examine face after face. There was nothing else to do. Now that he could survey them one by one, he was not sure they all were screaming in a frenzy of worship. When he looked at some faces, he saw that the mouths of humans could be brutal and animal, the tension in their throats, the dark holes of their gullets looking more like the maws of desert lions ready to tear him apart.

He began to wonder whether, out there in the crowd, there weren't also some scattered assassins who'd been planning to use the cover of the crowd to kill him.

He was outraged. Those bastards. Whoever they were.

How many would it take to attempt a coup? Ten. Maybe more. He had time, though: he would search the crowd until he found them.

For weeks, he scrutinized his people: methodically, in rows and columns, right to left, as scholars read the sacred texts. The faces out there bore the trace of countless different worries and concerns: for a son or a daughter, for a harvest, for a caravan that had not yet returned from far Khotan. Each one asking: *Will you be able to help?* Each one answering their own question: *No. You are only a weak man, mortal, ignorant, unable to move, just as we cannot move. Whatever we want, we will have to take. You can never know all that we demand, and what we will do to get it.*

Mouths open, shouting, angry fists raised. Perhaps the whole crowd hated him. He looked out at some grim hour (still surrounded by the constant chord of their applause), and he discovered that he actually feared the thousand thoughts he saw in different eyes.

Him—they despised *him*? This mob of the conquered, the humiliated, the toadies, the lackeys, the lickspittles, the slaves—and they despised *him*, the sultan of the Great Seljuqs, monarch over half the known world?

For several weeks after that he concentrated on projecting his hatred back out toward them, showing them he held them in complete contempt. He stood before them proud and strong, radiating a hate big enough to swamp them all.

It did not seem to affect them in the slightest.

They were stronger than he'd thought. As the months went by, he began to wonder how they would describe what they hated about him. What was their excuse? Sure, for some of them, he'd killed a husband, a father, a son in battle. But for the others?

They were sneering. They were sneering at him, a little goat-boy from the grasslands of the Khazars. A dirty little shepherd dressed up like a king of Persia.

What did they know about rulership that he did not?

Yes, some of them knew how to read. There were probably some princelings out there, some Persian scholars, some Arabic emirs, some imams out there who knew more than him about palaces and rituals and the history of kings.

He was sure now that they mocked him. They were not screaming in joy or rage. They were laughing at this stupid pageant. He was set before them, dressed like an idiot, a rustic fool they made parade in front of them on a little stage so they could howl.

He begged God to let him hide from the gaze of thousands, even just for a minute. *Let me go back through the doors. Let me go inside, and then you can freeze me again. Stop the noise just for a second. Please let there be silence. Let me stand in the dark.*

And so, hating himself, he stood through millennia upon his triumphal porch, glared at by his nation. *They hate me—they hate me— they can think of nothing else but how much they hate me.*

Some say the angels are full of eyes.

. . . .

For a full minute after his disappearance, the crowd was silent in shock. The balcony was empty.

Guards scrambled out of the palace, looking for him. Everyone gasped or started yelling.

But two hours later, people had gone back to their businesses and were throwing pots or selling sheep or counting amphoras of olive oil, saying, "You wouldn't believe it. He vanished, right in front of us. Snatched up by the angels." "Or the devils," someone else would say, and they'd laugh.

His disappearance didn't matter much. The throne wasn't empty for long. Two days later, a group of soldiers found a long-lost cousin from a minor branch of the Seljuq family in a tent near some fallen columns and hauled him to the city of Merv to declare him the new sultan.

By the time twenty years had passed, as Tuqshurmish in his bubble raged that everyone, everyone was consumed with an eternal hatred of him, he had actually been completely forgotten, or was remembered just as a kind of joke, called "the Fifteen-Minute Sultan." The weird little story of his disappearance was told in the *Malik-namah*, the history of the empire, an oddity taking up two sentences between more important matters (war, drought, God, dynastic marriage).

The crowd he had seen below him once he was suspended outside of time was only an image caught in his eye, of course. I didn't trap anyone else, because no one else that day, watching Tuqshurmish become sultan, had thought to themselves, *I wish this moment would last forever*. No one.

Except one irritating lackey toward the back, Ayyub. He was actually trapped with the sultan too, though they'll never know they're imprisoned together. Ayyub worshiped the sultan, and the crueler the man was, the more impressive Ayyub found him. Ayyub had been the one who'd personally strangled the sultan's fourteen-year-old brother on command the day before. After all, they had to tie up loose ends. As Ayyub stood in the crowd, looking up at his master—"I work for him," he boasted to the people around him, "I'm actually one of his most trusted servants"—he thought to himself, *Ah! Sultan Tuqshurmish! He's finally sultan! I wish this moment would last forever.* Ayyub was looking forward to a bright career of doing whatever he was told.

I should go to check on that asshole sometime. Maybe he's found out something about himself over the centuries. Jaw flapped open like the mouth of a trombone, blasting sound for all eternity. Nothing but a pipe of air screaming for an idiot king trapped on a stage, dreaming up stories of love and hate about people who have long ago turned to dust.

Margit, age twelve, Långviken, Sweden, 1953

This poor kid. Forever plunging down a hill on her bike, thrilled with speed. Summer night. Crickets in the fields around her. The sweet air in her face.

After an hour of that moment, the exhilaration turned pretty quickly to vertigo. She will never be at rest, because she will always feel the need to balance. She'll never stop falling forward.

None of us will.

Antoine-Armand, age seventeen, Lyon, France, 1724

This poor son of a bitch thought he looked suave in the silk frock coat and the crisp little wig he'd saved up for, and sure, he managed to convince his girlfriend to toss away the last mysterious barricade, but then, as they were working away at it there in the dairy, both panting, both taut, this blushing idiot wished the moment would last forever—in the fifteen seconds *before the shake hit him*. What kind of goddamn moron does that?

So he's hurtling forever toward fulfillment, but will never get there. Tendons all stretched. Nerves screaming. People don't usually think about the fact that there is very little difference between pleasure and pain.

He knows now: *Pure agony is just pleasure slowed down too far.*

He wishes he could scream, but his lips are in a grin.

Su Shan, ten years old, Hangzhou, China, 1992

Even the taste of your favorite cake nestled on your tongue, after a week, comes to seem like torture.

If you could choose, you would never eat it again.

Adefan, twenty-six years old, Kingdom of Aksum, Africa, 227

A father seeing his baby daughter for the first time. Don't ask to pause with her first yowl. Don't treasure it by begging time to stop. You deprive yourself of everything: the games in the mud, the endearments to animals, the hugs in the dawn, the lengthening of her limbs, the pride at her singing.

Your love is so great it has choked you.

You will never see her married. You will never see her children grow.

She will never weep to see you die.

And that is one of human life's great fulfillments.

· · · · · · · · · · · ·

Do you envy my collection? Do you wish that you could be preserved forever?

You may be mine at any time. Just think the words and I will come for you.

· · · · · · · · · · · ·

So boasts the demon Flaëlphagor.

He hates the human animal, and this is his revenge: these bright little gems of moments, these glittering souvenirs he rearranges, squinting at each one to savor its futility anew.

So he sits there for all eternity, trapped alone, cramped in a tiny cell near the lake of fire, unable to touch anyone, trapped without friends or lovers, bored to insanity, a hunched, pathetic little bat-winged mope. And this is why he sends his spirit out hunting through history: because the thing he hates most about the human animal is the way these mammals snuggle and the hope they share together. That is something he cannot stand.

Remember that, if you ever feel like him, recall him when you start to take pleasure in the suffering of the successful and the failure of the beautiful.

Remember the lesson of his awful collection of cameos: they show us how precious decay is, and loss, and the end of things sometimes. This is what makes our joy so poignant, because we cannot grasp forever the wrist we love, the streetlight's beam, the applause of friends, the air of summer, the speed of spoked wheels down a hill. This is why we wish they'd last forever, and why they absolutely should not.

Because you cannot truly love anything you will not someday lose.

Who We Are
What We Collect

M. T. Anderson (he/him) is the author of the satirical science-fiction novels *Feed* (winner of the Los Angeles Times Book Prize) and *Landscape with Invisible Hand* (which was made into a movie starring Tiffany Haddish and Asante Blackk). His Gothic novel of the American Revolution, *The Pox Party*, won the National Book Award. His short stories have appeared in several Year's Best Fantasy and Horror collections. His nonfiction writing has appeared in periodicals such as the *New York Times*, the *Washington Post*, *Slate*, and *Salon*. He lives in a small, haunted house in rural Vermont.

"I've always collected rare recordings of classical music. For example, as a teen, I collected requiem masses. (I was moody.) Sometimes I would try to collect all the different versions of one piece of music—or all the music ever written by a favorite composer. The composer Henry Purcell froze to death on his own doorstep at age thirty-six, after his wife locked him out. I decided to collect all the music he'd written by the time I was his age, when he died. Some of the pieces had never been recorded, though, so for my thirty-sixth birthday party, we sang the Uncollected Henry Purcell, all the forgotten pieces. Of course, in an age of streaming, that's all irrelevant, but it was an entertaining obsession at the time."

. . . .

e.E. Charlton-Trujillo is an award-winning author, filmmaker, youth literacy activist, and speaker who has written several books for teens and children, such as the ALA winner and Lambda Literary Finalist Fat Angie series; *Prizefighter en Mi Casa*; and their co-authored picture books with *NYT* bestseller Pat Zietlow Miller, *Lupe Lopez: Rock Star Rules!* and *Lupe Lopez: Reading Rock Star!*, illustrated by Joe Cepeda, and *A Girl Can Build Anything*, illustrated by Keisha Morris. A former Madrina in the Las Musas collective, Trujillo is also a cofounder of the nonprofit Never Counted Out. On and off the page, Trujillo strives to foster the desire/ganas in young people to celebrate their story and be heard. Find Trujillo online at eecharlton-trujillo.com or on the socials @pinatadirector.

> "It isn't by mistake that an adopted kid would collect things to fill
> in the gaps of their own story. Especially when their adopted story
> is so hard. Even now, I collect images, gadgets, pieces of machinery,
> recorded sounds, drumheads, ideas scrawled on crumpled receipts.
> Keys, coupons, books, handwritten notes, posters by Ernesto
> Yerena and Ray Scarborough. My office is full of found objects—
> shared objects—and sometimes my mind spins wild with the
> stories they've known. For me, objects witness some of our deepest
> secrets. Ensconced in their shapes isn't just their story, but ours."

. . . .

A.S. King is the author of more than a dozen novels that have garnered honors like the Michael L. Printz medal and the Los Angeles Times Book Prize—recent titles are *Dig, Switch,* and *Attack of the Black Rectangles.* She is a passionate advocate for teenagers, trauma-informed teaching, and singing loudly in her car. She lives in Pennsylvania.

> "I collect contemporary art, statues of Buddha, and most recently,
> small figurines of boys with squirrels."

. . . .

David Levithan is the author of a whole bunch of books, most recently *Answers in the Pages* and *Ryan and Avery*.

"When I was a kid, I collected ceramic tiles from the places my family visited. I had a fantasy of tiling a room with them— not necessarily a bathroom. Perhaps because of this, the tiles mysteriously disappeared from my parents' house."

. . . .

Cory McCarthy (he/they) is the author of bold, weird, and affectionate books. He studied poetry and screenwriting before earning an MFA at Vermont College of Fine Arts. Recently, Cory published the trans manifesto *Man o' War*, a Stonewall Honor book, a best of '22 at *Kirkus*, *BookPage*, Autostraddle, the Chicago Public Library, and BuzzFeed, as well as *Hope Is an Arrow*, a biography about fellow Arab American Kahlil Gibran, named a best of '22 by *Kirkus* and *School Library Journal*. He coauthored the bestselling King Arthur retelling *Once & Future*, a finalist for the New England Book Award, with his spouse, A. R. Capetta. Cory's books are in translation in over six languages, and he is sitting in a small yellow room in New England.

"Mostly I collected bad memories before I wrote this story. But I'm done with the pain of so much, the anger of it all. I reverse collect now. I say goodbye to scars. Evaporate them. Every time I light a candle or stare into a bonfire or at the sky—there another goes. I don't know what I'll collect next. I hope it's lighter than pain. I hope it's joy."

. . . .

Anna-Marie McLemore (they/them) is the author of William C. Morris YA Debut Award finalist *The Weight of Feathers*; *Wild Beauty*; *Blanca*

& *Roja*, one of *Time* magazine's 100 Best Fantasy Novels of All Time; Indie Next List title *Dark and Deepest Red*; *Lakelore*, an NECBA Windows & Mirrors title; and National Book Award long-list selections *When the Moon Was Ours*, which was also a Stonewall Honor Book; *The Mirror Season*; and *Self-Made Boys: A Great Gatsby Remix*. Their most recent novel is *Venom & Vow*, co-authored with Elliott McLemore.

> "My favorite collections are thanks to other people. Journals that friends gave me at just the moment I needed them. Passed-down aprons that turned my apron drawer into a proper collection. Ornaments from friends and family that adorn my tiny pink Christmas tree every year."

. . . .

G. Neri (he/him) is the Coretta Scott King Award–winning author of *Yummy: the Last Days of a Southside Shorty*, and *Ghetto Cowboy*, which was made into the movie *Concrete Cowboy*, starring Idris Elba, which debuted at number one on Netflix. His books have been translated into multiple languages in over twenty-five countries. They include *Tru & Nelle*, *Grand Theft Horse*, *Surf Mules*, *Knockout Games*, and *Chess Rumble*. Prior to becoming a writer, Neri was a filmmaker, an animator/illustrator, a digital media producer, and one of the creators of *The Truth* antismoking campaign. He writes full-time while living on the Gulf Coast of Florida with his wife and daughter. You can find him online at gneri.com.

> "Two things I collect: original art from all the amazing illustrators I've been privileged to work with on my sixteen books for young people, and . . . penguins. I spent two months on the ice in Antarctica, where I was known as the penguin whisperer due to my luck for penguin close encounters in the field. So I collect penguin figurines, toys, and dolls from around the world—the stranger, the better."

· · · · · · · · · · · ·

Jason Reynolds (he/him) is the author of more than a dozen books for young people, including *Look Both Ways: A Tale Told in Ten Blocks*; *All American Boys* (with Brendan Kiely); *Long Way Down*; *Stamped: Racism, Antiracism, and You* (with Ibram X. Kendi); *Stuntboy, in the Meantime* (illustrated by Raúl the Third); and *Ain't Burned All the Bright* (with artwork by Jason Griffin). He is the recipient of a Newbery Honor, a Printz Honor, an NAACP Image Award, and multiple Coretta Scott King Awards. Reynolds served as the National Ambassador for Young People's Literature from 2020–2022 and has appeared on *The Late Show with Stephen Colbert*, *The Daily Show with Trevor Noah*, *Late Night with Seth Meyers*, *CBS This Morning*, and *Good Morning America*. He is on the faculty at Lesley University, for the Writing for Young People MFA program, and lives in Washington, DC.

> "I collect all sorts of things. Art, especially by Black women, vintage timepieces, limited fountain pens, old Dupont lighters, rare first-edition books, well-designed wooden board games from around the world, ephemera from the civil rights era, letters from my friends and heroes, and hugs from my mother."

· · · · · · · · · · · ·

Randy Ribay (he/him) is the author of *Patron Saints of Nothing*, which won the Freeman Book Award and was selected as a finalist for the National Book Award, the Los Angeles Times Book Prize, and the CILIP Carnegie Medal. His other works include *An Infinite Number of Parallel Universes*, *After the Shot Drops*, and *Project Kawayan*. Randy was born in the Philippines and raised in the United States. He earned his BA in English Literature from the University of Colorado Boulder and his EdM in Language and Literacy from Harvard Graduate School of Education. He currently lives in the San Francisco Bay Area with his wife, son, and cat-like dog.

"In terms of the tangible, I mostly collect books—those I love, those I intend to read, those I hope my son will someday read, those written by fellow Filipino Americans. I also keep notes from students, letters from readers, and mundane items of emotional significance. As for the intangible, I use digital sticky notes to collect ideas, observations, questions, places, articles, quotes, interesting weather patterns, and favorite moments."

. . . .

Jenny Torres Sanchez (she/her) is a full-time writer and author of young adult novels and a picture book, and contributor to several essay and short-story anthologies. She was born in Brooklyn, New York, but has lived on the border of two worlds her whole life. Jenny's novels have won various awards and landed on several best-of lists, including *Kirkus*, *School Library Journal*, the New York Public Library, and more. Her most recent novel, *We Are Not from Here*, is a Pura Belpré Award book and is described by the *New York Times* as "a novel precisely for this moment." She lives in Orlando, Florida, with her husband and children.

"I collect small magical things—seemingly meaningless objects (rocks, buttons, candy, an origami crow) that somehow find their way to me and guide me to a story. I also collect vinyl because I'm a melomaniac. While working on 'Ring of Fire,' I carried in my pocket a matchbook with one match left inside and an ace of spades Johnny Cash playing card. I also listened to *The Essential Johnny Cash* on vinyl."